# The Tennis Racket

# The Tennis Racket

A Novella

Stuart Charles Neil

The Tennis Racket

Copyright © 2018 Stuart Neil

For Kate
(who founded the Childrens Home)

# ONE

"Get out, get out .......... Now.........this minute!
Take your clothes, your rackets, your damn orange balls
and your stupid hat and get out now! You are banned
from this Club. Don't even come within 100 metres
of it. I don't want to see your insolent face ever again.
Go........Go..........."

No one at the exclusive Malmo Tennisklubb had
ever seen the President so upset. In fact he had always
been the calmest person in their memory, and in any
crisis. Joel scampered around the court, collecting
tennis balls and belongings from three different places,
grabbed his bag and ran out of the gate. His friend,
Viktor, who had changed earlier, paused to let him go
by.

"I heard the crash. What the hell did you do?"

"Only broke a window"

"But you were practising serving – on the court, a
few minutes ago"

"Yeah. Well I was pissed off. I missed the ball box
three times in a row and smashed the next one at the
Clubhouse. Ha, ha. It went like a bullet straight at
Nosey's office window. Glass everywhere, all over his

desk. He leapt up, knocked over his coffee and then fell over the corner of his chair in a heap of papers and files and things."

"You stupid bugger. You know you were on a last chance."

"It wasn't intentional. I meant to slam it at the wall"

"You and your temper. That's about four warnings you have had?"

"Well I've got the push now and I don't give a shit. "

"Here's my bus." Viktor said. "Where are you going to play now Mr Joel Angers Eriksson?"

"It's Anders."

"Not any more. Angers by name, anger by nature."

Viktor climbed on the bus.

"Say that ever again and I'll break your neck" was Joel's parting remark.

He unlocked his bike from the wire fence beside Court Two, zipped up the bag and walked home pushing the bike the two kilometres to Nya Bellevue.


Joel was just fourteen and one of a group of promising young tennis players in Malmo. He could beat everyone under the age of eighteen amongst the Club Membership and had recently won the prestigious Kungens Kanna at the 'Swedish home of tennis', The Royal Klubb in Stockholm. This was for Boys under 14 years. He was on the radar as a fine prospect. He had many of the qualities needed to be successful in the professional game. Joel was strong for his age and had good stamina. His dedication to the sport was total. He practised and practised, playing matches at every opportunity. This was to the detriment of his schoolwork, which he was bright enough to pursue to a fairly high level. Joel spent most of each lesson clockwatching until it was time to go to the big Tennis hall at the Club as soon as the bell rang for the end of the school day.

The success in Stockholm and the praise heaped upon him, in front of his schoolfriends, by the Head-teacher and the Games Staff, his family and neighbours, coupled with new adulation from rapidly maturing girls, had gone to his head. Becoming the best junior player at the Club had begun the process a few months earlier. No-one likes an arrogant and rude teenager and Joel was both in quantity. Nobody seeks out the company of someone who only talks about himself and his own experiences, yet has no time to listen to theirs. The effect is the opposite to the encouragement and praise that he expects. Slowly but surely Joel became a 'loner' at school and an outsider from his peer group elsewhere.

In an attempt to look like the American tennis playboy, Vitas Gerulaitis, Joel grew his blond hair very long. The curls stretched out and they became lank and a bad example of the fashion. To keep it looking like his idol he needed to wash it almost every day. Of course he didn't. Once a week if the hair was lucky. Like many teenagers he had an untidy habit of walking stooped forwards looking at the ground. This meant that he passed teachers and other adults he knew without acknowledging them. He didn't care and frequently pushed through doors causing others to stand aside as he ploughed along regardless.

Joel had started playing tennis, hitting a ball against his home garage door, at the age of eight. He used a racket discarded by a cousin that, one day, he had found inside the same garage. His Father had died the previous year in a tragic accident at the Engineering Factory at which he worked. Mother Britt was in pieces and he and his little Sister, Anya, had just watched and cried with her. Months passed and the helpful neighbours reverted to their own lives, but one, Filip Nilsson, continued to assist by spending time with young Joel. Filip was one of the first of Sweden's tennis professionals when most players were amateurs and the pros had few tournaments and little money. Their main income came from coaching others.

Filip had no plan to introduce Joel to tennis. The little boy occasionally just went along with him when he was coaching other children. He pulled up one Saturday outside Britt's house and, over the low hedge, saw Joel knocking a ball against the solid wooden garage door. He stayed in the car and watched him hit ten......fifteen......twenty strokes without missing once. Forehand and backhand.....twenty-five........ thirty......then.., tap, tap.

The lady from across the road was knocking on the car window.

"Can you stop that boy from making that bang, bang noise, Mr Nilsson. It goes right through me. Every evening...bang, bang, bang. All weekend. If it was not for schooldays I would be in an asylum by now. His Mother says it keeps him out of mischief, but she doesn't get the migraine that there is in my family........"

From that day – Joel was eight years and four months old – he became Filip's most promising pupil.

Filip lost thousands of crowns of income by giving priority to a client who could pay nothing for the lessons. Joel became Filip's tail. He watched and learnt as much from watching others and helping the coach as he did from playing later on the same courts; Filip then teaching him instead of coaching 'paying' clients. Joel became a child star in a country hungry for new sporting talent.

During the next five years, and despite all the efforts of Filip Nilsson, Joel's head swelled and he became the 'spoiled brat' that everyone despised, copying the example of several of the top American players that he watched on television. Junior tournament Referees penalised him and he was twice disqualified from matches in an attempt to discipline his behaviour and rudeness. Then he discovered his temper; relieving his frustration by breaking equipment, verbally abusing linesmen and umpires and disrupting opponents. Filip began to withdraw his patronage, although he knew there was little chance of Mother, Britt, being able to curb her son's antisocial nature. Britt was totally occupied trying to hold the family finances together.

The Malmo Klubb was exclusive and the members paid a high annual subscription. Joel was there as a full tennis member on the recommendation of the Club's respect for Filip, their head coach. Joel always practised with orange tennis balls, one of his attempts to be noticed. The infamous temper caused these orange missiles, over a five week period one summer, to hit a motor cyclist on the adjacent main road, to knock over a buggy with a sleeping baby in it, to destroy a pyramid of profiteroles loving created as tea for a ladies

Wednesday Four and to poleaxe the Treasurer with a rocket between the eyes. The broken window was the final straw for the President, a kind and usually very tolerant retired baker. Lukas Eklund ('Nosey' to Joel for reasons only known to him, because Lukas had a pleasant shapely nose). He had decided, during a sleepless night the previous weekend that, whatever protests he received from the Tennis Federation or Joel's supportive fellow members, the very next misdemeanour would lead to permanent suspension or dismissal of this nasty child. Someone had to stop his behaviour on court and around the Club or he would turn out like McEnroe at his worst.

Viktor had suggested from the bus doorway that Joel would struggle to find anywhere to play. Municipal courts were few in Malmo and those that existed were fully used in the brief summer months. Also they were expensive and Joel had no money to spare. His concessionary membership to the tennis club had been free. For the rest of that summer the only court practise he managed was at school in Games lessons and after school until the janitor closed the gates. No one wanted to play with him or was good enough to knock up with him for long, even the Games and PE staff.

Filip had agreed with the Klubb President that it would be better to let Joel stew for a while and work out whether he wished to continue with tennis or stop playing altogether. Approaches from The Swedish Federation were deflected by Filip and they accepted that a change of behaviour was better for the future of the Country's tennis and needed as an example to other aspiring youngsters. Joel was allowed to enter tournaments, but found that, without quality practise, his success was limited. Miserably Joel watched Viktor win the Klubb tournament, beating one of the best of the Club's and the Region's men in the final. Viktor was also fourteen and, two weeks later, beat Joel in straight sets in the quarter final of an Under Eighteen Junior event in Gothenburg.

In August Lukas called Britt to ask whether he could come to the house and talk to Joel. When he arrived Joel was back at the garage door thumping fore and backhand groundstrokes against the thick wood. The house over the road had been put up for sale.

Lukas faced a glum teenager and told him that he had heard that his behaviour at school was acceptable (Joel conformed to most of the school rules in order to avoid detention at the end of the day, which would have encroached on his time to practise tennis.) He explained that if Joel was able to curb his temper and develop normal responses to others there was a chance that he (Lukas) would recommend resumption of his membership of the Malmo Klubb. It would be temporary, dependent upon exemplary behaviour, as he would like to see Joel succeed in the sport. Joel agreed.

Over the next two years, before the family moved to Gothenburg, Joel surprisingly made himself into the perfect Club Member. He nodded greeting to everyone, held open doors for his elders and, with great determination, began to accept that when things go wrong outbursts of temper never help to correct them. Like his passionate dedication to practise he devoted his thoughts to controlling emotion. Joel became silent!

Lukas and Filip said little but were amazed to

watch the internal battle going on inside the teenager. He developed an ice-cool temperament during games. No elation at a good shot, no outburst at an error. Attempts to distract his concentration by opponents failed. The only show of delight was when he won the match point, and even that was subdued.

The effect was slow on his peers and on the adults who knew him from before. They all imagined Joel would revert to type and say or do something bad in due course. He made new friends in the Club and at school. Growing in height and bulk and now washing his hair daily he became popular with more girls, new admirers. The cool exterior became even more attractive to them. He volunteered to be a waiter at the Tennis Club's Summer Dinner and Dance, cut his hair to be a little shorter and tidier and dressed in a black and white waiter's traditional uniform. Lukas just said "OK Joel ?" occasionally and enjoyed the Members' approval of their President's recommendation. The previously offended Members grew to like their young prodigy and were sad to see him leave to go to live in Gothenburg.

# TWO

At sixteen Joel won his way to the final of the Junior Singles tournament at Wimbledon. His cool temperament coped with larger crowds of spectators than he had encountered before. He lost the final to an Indian boy, who used guile and imagination to counter the first class groundstrokes of his opponent.

Filip had engaged the services of an Australian coach and used some of his own money to pay for this. The prize for 'Runner-up' in this prestigious tournament went towards this commitment, together with a supporting grant from the Swedish Tennis Federation. Filip felt that he now should play only a supportive role and that the coaching should be taken over by someone more familiar with the modern game. Darren had been prominent in tennis in Australia as a player and had coached three promising young girls since he qualified as a Tennis Instructor in Adelaide.

"You should never have lost that match. You're just not fit enough. It should have been a piece of piss to reach his drop shots and get closer to the drives to pass him at the net every time he came in." was Darren's response as Joel came into the Locker Room with the large shiny medal for second place that had been presented on Centre Court by the English Duke of Kent. Joel said nothing. Everyone else seemed pleased and his growing army of teenage fans ecstatic that he had progressed to the final from the position of 7th Seed.

Without complaint Joel pursued Darren's Fitness Plan. This involved a lot of running and swimming and a quite different diet to the one Joel had enjoyed back at home. His stamina improved and with it his alertness on court. However Darren never showed that he was pleased and constantly found reasons to put Joel down verbally. Often this was in front of friends or bystanders. Filip tried to curb the criticism, believing it to be corrosive to the confidence Joel needed to battle against tough opponents. Darren, however, told him that Joel could 'take it or leave it' in a blunt reply. Filip decided not to pursue the subject as Joel continued to progress well. Perhaps this was a successful technique that Darren had learnt from before or perhaps he was just jealous of the potential that Joel possessed, against the personal memory of himself reaching a limit of achievement in his mid-twenties.

"You're flat-footed again! Take off that stupid hat! Wear a sunshade instead. Where is the power in that shot? Keep running on the spot between rallies. Let's see if you can do it. Did you do more stretching this morning before you started? You'll not win anything worth while with that cold expression. Where's your passion? – an on and on. ............"

To Joel it became a drone that he seldom listened to on the surface. Filip contacted one of the fathers of Darren's previous pupils and found that they had finished the contract because his daughter was frequently in tears.

"We sent her for coaching because she loved to play and enter the junior events, but he took all the pleasure out of it for her and for us."

After one month's notice Darren returned to Adelaide and Filip resumed the coach's role. He needed a younger competitor as a 'sparring partner' for Joel who was too fast for his 55 year old body to cope with. Since losing to Samuraja at Junior Wimbledon Joel and Sammy had become firm friends. Sammy was the same age as Joel but came from a completely different background. He was a orphan from the South of India. Found by nurses he had been left near the bus stand outside the Aravind Hospital in Tirunelveli. This was not unusual in India where the social stigma of producing a baby as an unmarried mother was still very bad and there were few refuges to support a single mother and child. The nurses took him into one of the wards and kept him, taking it in turns to care for him during their meal breaks. He lay in a small metal cot that swung, like a hammock, attached to two metal posts that had wide feet planted on the floor. They kept him in the Staff Room until he became the first baby to be taken into a new charity home called 'Save the Babies' that had been started by a young girl from England in the same town. The transfer was approved by the Local Authorities and Sammy was visited frequently by the nurses, who had grown to love him.

Samuraja thrived in the Children's Home which grew to accommodate 32 children in one big, happy family. He did well at school and had been sent to an

English-Medium School. This was not an establishment for teaching people to become clairvoyant, but one in which every subject was taught in English, or South Indian English. English was regarded as the language to learn to be able to make your way in a wider world, and to find a job that would have a better prospect than one only available to a user of the local state language. Encouraged by the Houseparents at home Sammy began to play short tennis on a patch of land nearby, following success that Richard, the House Father, had had at Badminton and Kabbadi with other children. Sasees, his wife, was regarded by Sammy as his own Mother and she encouraged and enabled him to enter and win a number of tournaments in the south of the country.

Some of the international junior tournaments were operated in the same weeks as the senior events, so it was not long before Samuraja became invited as, quite often, India's only representative in the boys section of the latest tournament to be played. An enthusiastic India Tennis Association, together with his equipment sponsor, were thrilled at the opportunity to put sufficient finance behind their prodigy. The success of the Armitraj Brothers in the Grand Slam doubles category over the recent years, together with Vijay's starring role in the James Bond film 'Octopussy' had brought welcome attention to the limited sporting achievements of the world's second most populous country. The tennis contingent had always felt second best behind Cricket and Field Hockey and saw this as a chance to even things up.

The two of them, with Filip as mentor, and sponsored

by their respective national tennis associations together with equipment manufacturers, played in tournaments around the world. They won and lost, gaining experience and learning much about themselves in the process. They roomed together to economise until each began to earn winnings to supplement the support fees paid by the sponsors. During the days in between events they practised together, learning from each other and the wealth of skills that were still locked inside Filip's tennis brain. He didn't try to find another coach for them after the Darren experience. Sammy had never had an official coach, having listened and learnt his art from a variety of contacts, and making friends and watching every better player he could find. This included hours watching videos of close matches, which he borrowed from television companies and played in his room. Joel began to do the same until they each decided to model parts of their game on specific players. Joel idolised Stefan Edberg and Sammy became a clone of Jimmy Connors.

Samuraja was conditioned in the Indian correctness of spending very little time with members of the opposite sex during the teens and twenties until the family broached the subject of marriage. He remained reluctant to get close to any of the admiring hoard of attractive females who spent fruitless hours watching through the wire netting around the courts of the world, only very occasionally going out with a girl. Joel, however, was neither celebate nor inhibited by a national habit of separating boys and girls at the point of maturity. The Swedes had a reputation for being exponents of free love, a concept more than attractive to the equally free thinking western girls of these times. Mixed schools enabled children in Sweden to grow up together and to be unafraid of light or heavy commitments. Those who preferred the prospect of blond boyfriends made their presence obvious behind the courts that Joel practised on.

The two guys frequently discussed the advantages and disadvantages of developing close relationships with the girls who seemed to appear at every opportunity. Each respected the others angle on this with Joel constantly out to widen his portfolio and Sammy reserving his favours for the prospect of a happy marriage when the time came. Sammy had already beaten Joel in the Wimbledon final of the Boys singles. He continued to have the upper hand throughout the next year. Filip had a theory that Samuraja was gaining in strength and competitive edge because he kept to a routine of fitness and early nights, whereas Joel was frequently partying until late with the current girlfriend.

At nineteen, however, Joel grew an extra two inches in height. This was late for even a boy and it made him surprisingly stronger than he had been before, and taller than Samuraja. It did wonders for his service, which became the principal shot of his armoury. He began to move up the rankings of the elite male singles players by beating those higher on the list. Although he had not yet won a major tournament he was reaching quarter and semi finals on a regular basis. It increased his confidence and his income in equal proportion and he reached No 17 in the world rankings, qualifying him to entered every tournament he wished and usually to be seeded.

Filip's death was totally unexpected. He collapsed with a heart attack in his room in Hong Kong and had died before anyone found him. Both Sammy and Joel were devastated. Joel, in particular, because Filip had not only steered him through his teenage woes but had been a father figure for as long as he could remember. He had planned Joel's complete tennis programme of events, equipment, practise and diet. Sammy was more independent and coped better with the loss. In one year Joel's ranking fell outside the top fifty whereas Sammy continued to hold his level and rise three places.

Although the tennis press continued to give Joel the benefit of the doubt he was stepping nearer to obscurity, after having been the glamour boy of the future in every article and on advertising hoardings. One spell found him not winning through the first round of five consecutive tournaments. The pair had appointed a new coach and a new, experienced management team. Joel struggled to identify with any of them and began missing training sessions.

In Singapore he was approached by a suspicious character called Oscar, who told him he could make a lot of money gambling on tennis matches. Not using his sense Joel listened. They were in the main airport at the time en route to Shanghai and, due to his recent failures, money was on Joel's mind. He was beginning to wonder whether his meagre earnings were covering expenses. Apparently all he had to do was win or lose matches to Oscar's order and his contacts would pay him in dollars. When pressed Oscar revealed that these contacts were operating near where they were sitting, but would link with him anywhere on the globe. People in the Far East will gamble on anything and it seemed that tennis results were the latest topic. The syndicate would offer better than usual odds on a result and, depending upon the amount the punter stood to lose, Oscar would advise Joel to win or throw the match. He, Joel, would have to go on a winning streak before they would consider him now because of his poor recent results, although they were prepared to run a trial when he played someone good this year and managed to win.

In a rash moment Joel showed Oscar the draw for the Shanghai event next week. If Joel won through the first round he would meet the seeded Greg Rusedski, who would be an odds on favourite. Oscar made a phone call and returned to say that they would pay him US$5,000 if he won that match. They had no intention of laying special odds but, unknown to Joel, wanted to check his integrity. If he won they would realise that he could turn on his form as if there was a switch. Joel knew that Filip would have bawled him out for even considering this. They moved on to Shanghai and Joel managed to beat his first round opponent in straight sets.

Greg Rusedski was good on a wood surface, which used to be the floor of this stadium. However they had laid a new carpet and it was playing a lot slower than expected. This was Greg's first match as he had a bye with his seeding. Joel won the first set easily at 6-2 using the first round experience playing on the surface. Using his service strength Greg won the second set 7-5, and after a titanic struggle also the third 7-5. Joel was worried in case the syndicate decided to send some heavies to punish his inability to conform to the instructions given. Oscar appeared and took Joel to one side, telling him that, although they were unhappy, he had made a great effort so they could not fault his intention. He didn't mention that the syndicate had not lost any money on this trial arrangement.

Content that they now had someone they could rely on Oscar got down to the real reason they needed Joel's co-operation. It was not the winning and losing of matches that made the real money in Far Eastern gambling. It was what is called 'spot betting' that the wealthier clients would stake the largest sums on. In his next tournament Joel was asked to perform a specific task at a particular point in the match. Joel's match was being used for a variety of bets, most of which he would have no idea about. They were the ones when the punter would win, those when the bets were small and wins were allowed to keep the gambler happy. It was the point when a high stake had been laid that he had to perform. For example, serving a double fault in a certain game – something he rarely did, or re-tying his shoe lace after the first point of his opponent's service game.

Joel had been reluctant to continue the win/lose arrangement but was willing to go along with a single point instruction as he didn't feel it lost the integrity of his tennis. Over three months he made US$50,000, which was paid to him in bundles of local currency. He then went to a local Bank and changed the notes into dollars.

Early in the season there was a rumour that one of the gamblers had become suspicious of losing too often and persuaded someone in the gang to give away the method. The Tennis Authorities heard of this and began an investigation. Joel became one of a short list to be interviewed. It seemed as though the message had only come through about throwing matches and the one involving Joel was the Rusedski encounter, which Joel had nearly won. He was above suspicion and mightily relieved. Just before the grass court season began Joel told Oscar that he no longer wanted any part of the scam and refused any further involvement. An annoyed Oscar had made a strange parting remark:-

"I think you will decide to continue my friend."

Oscar made several attempts to contact him again, but each time Joel refused to even speak with him.

# THREE

"Snails are not a standard part of a sportsman's diet" said Samuraja to the waitress in the competitors café at the Eastbourne Tennis Tournament.

"It's not a snail, Sir. It's a slug."

"OK. But what if I was a vegetarian?"

"It's not really meant to be in the salad."

"Are you sure? I mean, I thought it was a bonus because this is the third time this week I have eaten in this exclusive establishment."

"No, really really. I'll take it back and bring you a fresh one"

"I don't need a fresh slug. This one looks delicious".

"Stop it Sammy. She is already embarrassed enough serving you. And all her friends are watching." Joel chipped in.

Sammy smiled at the girl. She was only about 16 and probably moonlighting at the café during her time off between GCSE exams.

Polly (it said on her badge) took the plate and fled to the kitchen.

It was always pot luck which of the pre-Wimbledon grass tournaments to enter in order to get in some serious practise on the change of surface after the clay court season. This year Joel and Samuraja had been urged by their sponsors to come to Eastbourne in the South East of England. Although they both entered the Men's Singles competition it was the doubles that they really wanted practise at, having recently decided to pair up and play together.

Inevitably, both being single and good looking, there were small groups of girls and women in the vicinity apparently occupied with their various conversations but finding it necessary to keep looking in the general direction of the two men eating lunch. Each was 21 years old. Samuraja was now six feet tall, very dark skinned as were many of his countrymen in Tamil Nadu, South India. He was slim with short, dark hair, a ready smile and strong muscular legs that were visible as he sat in his tennis gear set off with a black zipped-up jacket sporting the Nike tick logo. Joel, in contrast, was blond with long, curly hair that looked as if it never had, nor ever needed the Afro comb that lived at the bottom of his Yonnex tennis bag. He was two to three inches taller than Sammy and had bronzed arms and legs that were covered with a half-inch mat of hair that would not have looked out of place on a golden retriever.

The Tournament lasted a week and this was Thursday. It attracted a good number of the top players, men and women, and was eagerly awaited by the residents of the town and most of Sussex. Although Joel expected to be, Sammy was surprised to find himself still in the singles event because he was rated outside the top 50 this year. He regarded himself as more of a doubles player now on the International Tour, many of whom made a good living from their skills of being able to play in harmony with another, either male in Doubles or female in Mixed Doubles. He also enjoyed the reduced pressure of Singles. When ranked higher, losing a match he should have won, it would provoke an inquest amongst his coaching team and the tennis press. Having won his third match of the week this morning he enthusiastically attacked the seafood salad that Polly had now replaced.

Joel was not eating as he was due on court as soon as a ladies single match completed, and should really have been loosening up on one of the eight practice courts that lay in a row in the middle of the complex. An official came and told him that this match had now gone to a third set, so he ordered a drink and remained with his friend in the café.

"What is all this about someone writing a book about you ?" asked Sammy with his mouth full.

Joel looked away and didn't answer immediately.

"The word on the street is that it is to be' the autobiography of the decade' with more revelations than the reader could find in last Sunday's newspapers."

"Mmmm" came the reply.

"Come on, tell me. I don't want to have to buy the wretched book." Joel hesitated as Sammy demolished another huge forkful of lettuce, peppers and prawns.

"It's another of those 'tell me about your life and I'll sell a million copies' offers"

"I wouldn't mind having just one of those." added Sammy.

"This one is odd. A vast amount upfront before I am supposed to utter a word, and a total fee and royalties that is way beyond any of the others, and I think too good to be true. What is even more odd is that it's Lindsay who is acting for the publisher. Oh, God, here she comes now."

Lindsay was in her mid twenties and had been playing the tournament circuit for five years until retiring recently to work as a junior reporter on the tennis scene, sending her reports and interviews to the editor of a magazine that is sold in several countries. Joel and Sammy both knew her and she and Sammy had visited a few restaurants together two years ago during the US Open, when they had played together in mixed doubles.

Lindsay was slim, blonde and was weaving her way through the tables, pointedly heading in their direction, her hair blowing across her face and causing her to collide with one of the waitresses.

Joel finished his drink and stood up as if about to leave.

"Joel, don't go. I need a decision today."

He sat down again. Lindsay continued talking to him in her soft New Zealand accent without acknowledging Sammy's presence.

"Have you made your decision yet?" she fired at Joel.

The table of young players next to them stopped talking and some turned their heads to see who was addressing these popular guys so aggressively.

"Not yet." replied Joel "I am due on court in a moment and need to warm up first". He stood up again. "Why don't you ask Sammy here? His life is much more interesting than mine and he needs the money to keep his Harem happy."

The next table seemed unable to resume their conversation.

"But my Publisher insists you have to decide now."

"Tell your Publisher I will let you know before the tournament finishes."

He picked up his sunglasses and headed out of the café, followed by Lindsay.

One of the middle-aged volunteer linesmen (linepeople) came over from her table, sat down and faced Sammy.

"Hello, I'm Helena. Tell me about your Harem......... where is it?"

Behind dark rimmed glasses an intense look of belief shone from her green eyes so convincingly that Sammy couldn't resist replying.

Aware that he also had an audience he told her about his Estate just outside Bengaluru in South India where he bred horses on a small scale. This was true. He told Helena, who began making notes in a bright blue notebook, that it was a cover for the Harem that he was building up of young women of a number of nationalities. It was against the law in India these days but lots of rich men still did it. They were all exceptionally pretty girls, who came from poor families and whose fathers could not afford a dowry large enough to buy a good husband.

"How do you find them?" Helena questioned

The ears behind Sammy were not sure about this but decided to listen to more. They hardly knew Sammy either; he having competed at different events to most of them.

"I pay agents to roam the Far East in countries

where the dowry is one of the pillars of culture. Now, I notice you are not wearing a ring. Is there a dowry culture in your country?"

Helena ignored the audible snigger from behind Samuraja and turned a significant shade of red. Even her glasses seemed to change colour.

"No, no. definitely not. I am from Wales, where we are very civilised."

"This is quite civilised." Sammy continued. "It is just a different culture. In fact our civilisation was established long before yours. When you Welsh were running up and down the mountains half naked and sticking spears into each other Tamils were educated and cultured."

Helena regained her composure.

"It must be expensive to keep several women. How many do you have?"

"Eighteen now and another two on the way."

There was a spluttering sound from behind as someone was having a problem drinking her smoothie.

"What do you do with them all?

Sammy paused and looked at her.

"I'm sure there will be a book about it somewhere in the Eastbourne Library if you look hard enough"

The pinky red colour re-appeared, this time around her neck and chin.

"I manage to keep the party going with all my winnings from tennis, and refraining from buying expensive cars and houses around the world."

"Do you come from one of the rich Indian families?"

Sammy went on to tell her that he was from a 'Backward Cast' and his family was very poor. At the time of the British Raj they were punka wallas.

One of the girls from the table behind said "Sorry, I have been listening. Did you say 'punk rockers'?" The others laughed.

Sammy explained that a punka was a large piece of canvas attached to a lightweight plank of wood suspended from the ceiling, from which stretched a thick string which went out through the window or a hole in the wall. The 'punka walla' sat outside with the other end of the string tied around his big toe. He bent and stretched his leg pulling the string and causing the canvas to swing back and forth in the inside room moving the heavy humid air around and relieving the heat burden of the overworked British officials and their Memsahibs. Hard work on the legs and feet.

"My Great Uncle was famous in Bengaluru in the 1930's and in great demand because he had been made 'pukka punka walla of 1936', a title coveted by many Indians and he was sought after by the perspiring Brits."

There was a growing scepticism at the next table, with one of the men having to leave to avoid laughing out loud. Meanwhile Helena took copious notes and concentrated upon Sammy's every word.

"Sadly, all the jobs had gone by the time I was born, so I was in danger of having no choice but 'coolie work' when I left school. In fact we were so poor that I began pulling carts at the age of ten to earn enough for the family to eat. The punka walla was cast out of employment by two things; electricity and ceiling fans. But a miracle came over the horizon. After independence some of the Brits unexpectedly stayed on in India and they, the Anglo-Indians and the new wealthy Indian leaders and government officers began to have spare money and to discover relaxation. The 'hammock' appeared in every garden, hanging in the shade of a big tree. There was as yet no machine invented to rock a hammock."

He glanced behind at the girl who had spoken earlier.

"India never had 'punk rockers' or even 'punka rockers' but my friends and I moved on to become 'hammock rockers'. Legends in our own lifetime. The system was similar to the punka. String tied to one side of the hammock and me sitting on the ground ten metres away behind a tree in case I should hear any conversation my employer was having".

"How long did you do that?" asked Helena, thinking that she had a good story to write and send to a tennis magazine.

"About 10 hours a day at 8 rupees an hour. 6 or 7 years and I had enough to go to College and learn tennis. However it has left me with a major problem. The big toe on each foot is now an inch longer than all the others. It means I have to wear special tennis shoes that are very expensive. It is also why I am good at Doubles. You see, when it is my turn to serve, the extra long toe helps me to push off from the baseline like a spring. I reach the net beside my partner in two strides and can volley a winner with ease."

Helena was still writing. Sammy stood up and shook his head at the group behind and put a finger to his lips.

"Head the article 'The Hammock Rockers of Bengaluru' and send the fee to my Manager."

He got up and walked out of the café followed by five others, quietly laughing into their hands, leaving an enthusiastic Helena scribbling alone.

# FOUR

Lindsay was frightened! Two days earlier she had had a scary experience.

Having completed a short course in journalism she had only recently begun a job with the magazine 'Slam'. She had been sent to Eastbourne to cover the week and write gripping articles on the competitors. Whilst interviewing some of the players on Sunday and Monday she had become aware of two men watching her. She would not have noticed once or twice, but four times seemed unsettling. As her interviews had been with different players she concluded that they were particularly interested in her.

Having parked her Clio in a side street well way from the tennis to save parking charges she made her way towards it late on Monday evening. It was still light at 9pm on this, one of the longest days of the year. Zigzagging through the streets towards her car she approached a junction. Suddenly the two men who had been at the tennis stepped around the corner in front of her.

"Lindsay?"

"Er Yes. What do you want?" Startled, she stepped back.

"We want to offer you a contract. Come into the pub here and meet Nor."

She noticed there was The Crown Pub right beside them.

"I have to get home and write up my day's interviews."

"It will only take a few minutes and Nor is anxious to meet you."

The pub was busy with music playing and a general hubbub of conversation. She thought for a moment.

"OK. But ten minutes maximum."

They walked through the door and the place was packed. The men pushed a channel past people standing three deep at the bar. They headed towards the far wall. A woman waved. When they reached the table at which she was sitting Lindsay noticed that she had been keeping the other three chairs vacant.

"This is Nor." said one of the men. "I am Oscar and this is Rayyan."

"You must be wondering what this is all about." said Nor. "We have a little proposition to put to you, using your journalist skills. But let me get you a drink first."

"I can't stop. I must get home and work on my interviews for the day."

"Just one drink whilst we talk. Rayyan will get them."

"I am driving. Orange and lemonade please."

Rayyan set off into the crowd at the bar.

"Lindsay, we want you to befriend Joel Eriksson and make him a proposition on our behalf."

"Why me? Why can't you do it?"

He only talks to pretty women and you have a 'Press' pass into the player's areas.

"I'm not pretty and I wear glasses these days."

"The boys here reckon you are easy on the eye. And his last girlfriend wore specs."

"What do you want me to do?"

"The important thing is to befriend him now. We'll tell you more later. Offer him a lot of money to write his life story and, when he agrees, begin to take notes in your normal reporter's method."

"I already have a job and am busy this week."

"We want you to stay near him this week and all the time until the end of the Wimbledon Fortnight."

"Sorry, I can't do it. My editor will have loads of different tennis work for me in the next weeks." Lindsay stood up to leave.

"Sit down. There is a great offer for you in this."

She reluctantly sat again as Rayyan appeared with drinks for all four.

Nor looked left and right to check who may be listening.

"One thousand pounds now and another four thousand in a month at the end of the contract." said Nor almost under her breath.

Lindsay sat back in her chair for a moment, and then forward again to take a long drink from the tall glass in front of her. Her annual salary was only £15,000 as a new reporter. Four months salary to talk to an attractive man about his life in a few visits between his matches here and at Wimbledon. It would be a dream for most reporters, young or old.

"You will need to take leave from your current job

to do it – just three weeks." This was Oscar joining the conversation.

"No, sorry. I can't do that. I have only been with the magazine since Easter. There is no way I can get time off until October, after the tennis season finishes."

Nor looked across at Oscar and Rayyan, who shrugged his shoulders.

She looked serious and a little menacing when she said

"Don't be sorry. We are sorry that we have to insist. This is very important to us and we can't take 'no' for an answer."

Lindsay picked up her bag and file of papers and made to leave, glad that there were many others in the pub and that they were not alone..

"Thank you for the offer, but I must go now."

She pushed her way through the throng and reached the door. Looking back she began to wonder what the meeting was really about; a bad premonition beginning to creep into her mind. She noticed Oscar stand up and look at her and start to move in her direction. Pushing open the door she stepped out into the street and hurried off in the direction of her car. Reaching it around two more corners she found her keys and jumped into the driving seat, selecting the ignition and starting the engine in one movement with relief. Before the Clio could pull out from its space between two other parked cars there was a tapping at the window and Oscar's face appeared. She tried to drive away but the little car needed to move back and forth once more to clear the Toyota in front. Oscar had quickly run around to the passenger side, opened the door and sat in the seat next to her

'Damn, I should have locked the doors' she thought, too late.

"Switch off for a minute" he said calmly.

Lindsay hesitated.

"What do you want? I've told you I cannot accept the offer."

"You will do exactly what Nor has said. I don't give a shit about your job. We will pay you well and you can get another job soon enough."

She pulled back in her seat in shock at the aggressive way he spoke.

"Meet me by the Vegetarian Snack Stall at the tennis tomorrow at 10am sharp and I will give you your next instructions. We will be watching you. Don't talk to anyone else about this – Police, friends, relatives, anyone !! We know where you are living, so don't let us down."

"Why are you threatening me ? This is some sort of crime isn't it?"

"Just don't, is all I can say."

"You don't know where I live – you are just trying to frighten me."

Oscar climbed out of the car. Before closing the door he leant in and said

"22 Connaught Drive, Hove. Your Mother seems quite nice, but you shouldn't leave her alone all day. Bet you love the dog too."

He closed the door and walked away.

Lindsay put the car in gear and drove out of the town. She looked in the mirror several times but no-one seemed to be following. Steering with her left hand in between changes of gear she tried to stop her other hand from shaking. After a mile she pulled into the forecourt of a filling station, parking away from the pumps, and sat looking through the windscreen gripping the steering wheel in both hands and staring ahead.

* * * * *

The first competitors, umpires and linesmen were making their way out to their allotted courts the next morning in bright sunshine. The two ladies operating the Vegetarian Snack Stall had opened its shutter. They were not expecting any serious business for another hour and were busy at the back work surface washing fruit and cutting tempting slices of kiwi and pineapple to put in small polythene trays. One of them broke from her conversation to serve Lindsay with a white coffee.

It was five to ten and Lindsay had slept only fitfully last night. Unable to sleep at all after 5am she pulled a coat over her pyjamas and went out into the garden. The bungalow was on the gentle slope of a hill and the front garden overlooked other houses and the sea a few hundred yards away. The sun was already well above the horizon to the East. She had bought the bungalow with her saved tennis winnings to enable her Mother to move to England and be near her sister, whilst going through a temporary separation from Lindsay's Father in Otago, New Zealand.

Her thoughts were a little more ordered this morning after a late evening and parts of the night sitting or lying in a turmoil. Without a criminal thought in her mind for 21 years she now found herself drawn into some plan or scam that she didn't understand and definitely wanted no part of. She had been threatened with 'heaven knows what' if she did not conform to the bidding of the sinister trio in the pub. And the prospect of her Mum, or even Vanilla her lovely Labrador, being harmed was very worrying. She dare not go to the Police. Anyway, they would laugh at her.

"What is the crime, Madam?" "I don't know."

"So they were watching you and then they bought you a drink." "Yes."

"You are an attractive female. Even I may have done that. With no crime intended."

"If we asked them whether they threatened you or your Mother or your pet, is it likely any of them would admit it?"

The Police would say they couldn't give her any protection because there was no proof that she was not just paranoid, and their resources were overstretched anyway. The trio would be watching and take out their vengeance on her or worse, her family.

Lindsay decided that she had no option but to go along with the task they wanted her to do. It was a weak reason that they couldn't do it themselves because they didn't have Press passes and couldn't come near enough to Joel Eriksson to strike up a conversation. Maybe he knew them and disapproved their tactics or knew they had criminal records. Also, what could be so secretive about an autobiography. It must have some sensational elements if it was worth such a lot of money to them. Enough to offer her five thousand pounds and a pile to him in advance for the story.

At that moment Joel walked past her with his opponent and a posse of ball girls, umpire and line officials. She caught her breath at his good looks, long blond hair kept in check with a headband. The two ladies behind the stall counter had stopped and were looking, one holding a knife and half an orange in one hand and the second half in the other dripping juice on the floor. Her mouth was partially open as if in mid-sentence. They didn't need to say anything and Lindsay agreed with the unspoken thought. She turned around to find herself standing face to face with Oscar !

He was wearing a royal blue tee shirt, navy shorts and trainers and looking less like a tennis player, more like a runner in the geriatric section of the London Marathon.

"Decided to join us?" he asked.

"Only because you give me no choice." Lindsay replied, hardly opening her mouth to spit out the words.

"Perhaps this will help." He handed her a brown plastic bag folded around what appeared to be a bundle of notes.

She gingerly took the bundle and, without opening it, pushed it inside her small shoulder bag.

"Go to him between matches. He has a routine. Showers, changes and always comes out into the competitors cafe. He is a friendly bastard and knows everyone on the main circuit. He will grab a cup of black coffee, or maybe you will buy him one as an introduction. Catch him alone. He will like you. His last girlfriend wore specs rather than contacts. He used to sit directly opposite her, take off her glasses and kiss her on the nose. Try letting him do the same."

"Huh. Some chance. I'll bet she was some skinny supermodel."

"No. An umpire actually."

"Oh, yes. I remember – she was on the circuit with the rest of us last year."

"Pay attention. This is the important part. You are representing a new publisher, which has strong investment backing and needs a stunning book to announce its presence on the world publishing stage. You want his autobiography. You can offer him 250,000 Euros to sign a contract to do it. Then 500,000 Euros on publication with 10 per cent of all sales proceeds indefinitely."

"Isn't it rather early to be writing an autobiography when you are 24?"

"21. He is 21. Believe me, there is enough for two books. And that is what we already know. You will be able to find out more."

"I don't really know how to get the best out of him. I am only a trainee journalist a few months into the job. I've never written a book, let alone one that is personal. I played – up to last year anyway – but I was only on the fringe of his circle.. He never showed any interest in me."

"Use all your feminine guile. You know. Find out what he likes and give it to him. Don't be too serious about him. Sleep with him."

"Do you mind? I am a respectable girl, not some high class prostitute."

"Up to you. You'll need to be good at something to find out all the hidden secrets."

He walked away, just like he had done the previous evening.

Lindsay made her way to the court allocated to Joel for his singles match and used her Press Card to gain entry into the cramped front section amongst the photographers. She watched the whole of the first set, which he won despite losing his first service game. Then she decided to make her way to the Competitors Café where she could wait for him to show up after his customary shower and also watch the Master Scoreboard. This would help her decide who else to interview on behalf of the magazine if she was to have any chance of keeping her job.

Joel appeared on cue, having lost the match in three sets that he should have won. He looked depressed. She took Oscar's suggestion and bought a cup of black coffee, placing it in front of him before the waitress could reach his table.

"You are a lot of trouble. Why don't you get back on court instead of hanging around with the Press ?" said Joel.

"Given up tennis. I was no good anyway."

"Thought you won a couple of tournaments two years ago."

"Downhill since then."

"What is this book offer then ? Can't be serious."

"Why not?"

"Silly money. No publisher could afford that for a book on me"

He asked her what she would need to know and in what detail. It seemed she was not sure, so he became more suspicious.

"Your editor is not called Nor, is she?"

"Er…. There is a Nor involved"

"What a co-incidence! This Nor has been leaving messages for me to contact her, but there has been no mention of a book. I have been having a problem with a group of people in the Far East and Nor is an Eastern girl's name."

"My instinct is to say 'No' unless you can throw more light on all this."

Lindsay leant closer.

"Do you know anyone called Oscar?"

"Now you are making sense. Yes, I know Oscar."

Lindsay told him the whole story of how she had been threatened and was scared. If Joel gave her away they would do bad things to her and possibly her Mother.

"There is more to this than you realise. I'll keep quiet about most of it, save to tell you that it is a gambling scam to get players to play below their standard. I need to go to the loo. Stay here and I'll be back in a minute."

Thinking whilst he was in the loo he made a decision.

"If we don't play along with this they will be around for months. Let's play along and set them up in some way."

"I don't understand."

"We'll set them up to be caught. Not obviously, but accidentally in some way."

"But they are dangerous and will get revenge."

"Only if they think we did the setting."

"We'll have to be very careful."

"Go back and tell them I agree to the terms for the book and I'll meet you here tomorrow."

This had been earlier in the week and Joel told

Lindsay to keep a pretence in public that she was trying hard to persuade Joel to agree to the book offer. Hence the later meeting in the open restaurant area with Sammy and his Harem story.

Joel went straight to the Police Station in Eastbourne and asked to speak to a senior detective. Detective Inspector Gareth Williams was in his office catching up on paperwork. Joel explained as much as he knew about the gambling scam and the threat to Lindsay. Williams agreed to lend Joel a miniature microphone and tape recording machine on a promise that the evidence was returned to him only and that the Press did not become involved.

The next day Joel and Sammy were knocked out of the doubles. Much of the blame should have fallen in Joel's lap as he lost his service game each time through the match, which was against opposition that they had beaten before. Joel's enthusiasm for tennis was waning rapidly. He met Lindsay in the same place and, under the cover of the edge of the table, showed her the tape machine.

"Can you wear loose clothes when you meet them and obscure this little recorder? Put the microphone and lead inside your shirt which is fortunately nearly the same colour and that won't be seen either. Switch it all on just before you meet their representative. Here is a list of questions to ask them. The answers will reveal their guilt, so my police friend tells me."

"If they find out what I am doing they may kill me."

"Murder carries a much bigger penalty than illegal gambling. More likely they will destroy the evidence and send you packing. Try to meet up in a crowded place so they cannot be violent."

Lindsay hesitated but eventually agreed and met Oscar this time in a shelter on Eastbourne seafront. Nor and Rayyan were both there and wasted no time in describing their ploy to get Joel to resume his spot betting arrangements by playing on his concerns for Lindsay's safety if he did not. They emphasised their methods of dealing with contacts who did not perform the letter of their instructions and showed Lindsay a photograph of one man with a missing arm, whom they claimed was a victim. They were confident that Joel would play along and gave her a card with three specific tasks he had to perform during tomorrow's mixed doubles match when he was playing with his current partner Monika.

Policeman Gareth Williams commended Lindsay upon acquiring the tape and began working with his counterpart police force in Malaysia. He suggested that Joel did exactly what he had been instructed so that no suspicion could be traced to him or Lindsay if the scammers were caught. Joel served two double faults in his second service game, changed his tennis shirt between the first two sets and played more than six lobs over the net player during the match. It was difficult for he or the Detective Inspector to believe that gamblers were prepared to bet on such obscure items.

The next meeting for instructions was communicated to Lindsay to be back in the Crown Pub, where she had first heard of the scam and her forced inclusion. The police waited outside in an unmarked van so as not to implicate Lindsay in their decision to arrest the three crooks. They waited until she had left and then wasted no time in going in to pick up the trio. This coincided with Oscar buying drinks at the bar. He watched the police pass by, realised that the game was up and dived into the toilet.

The window was quite a large one. Oscar opened it and climbed out into a side street and managed to avoid the police altogether.

Nor and Rayyan were identified as being illegally in the country and both had criminal records in Singapore with Nor also known in Malaysia. They were charged from the evidence of the tapes and a partial confession from Rayyan, who was anxious to avoid being deported to Singapore. There was apparently very little on the tape to incriminate Oscar. The police decided to stop looking for him. Meanwhile the tennis circus moved on to Queens Club in London for the annual grass tournament there. It was not long before the trial came to Court as the evidence for the prosecution was straightforward. Two weeks after the end of the Wimbledon fortnight Nor and Rayyan were both sentenced to four years in jail for their part in corrupting competitive tennis and, at the same time, the Lawn Tennis Association began an investigation into how many other such scams had been in operation in England. Joel, in the middle of the worst tennis performance of his life to date, found himself and Lindsay central to their enquiries and having to attend, under oath, meeting after meeting with tennis officials and solicitors, all chaired by a retired judge. Several times they came close to finding that Joel had been involved with the gang before, and there were some unpleasant suggestions in the tabloid press with photos of Joel printed next to each one..

Lindsay was unable to use the story in her capacity as a tennis reporter due to restrictions placed upon publicity by the judge chairman. She had decided anyway that she would return to New Zealand, leave all this behind her and get as far away from Oscar as possible in case he took revenge on her. There was nothing to suggest her involvement in the arrests but she did not feel free of all implications. For some time she had been contemplating going home to train as a PE teacher and to check that her Father was coping now he was alone. Joel was ready to take a 'sabbatical' from tennis as some others had done in the past. A clean break for a few months would give him a vacation and a chance to put his recent trail of bad results behind him. He thought it may be like some of the women players did – take a break, have a baby, return after a year happier and enjoying a return to fitness.

# FIVE

"Lindsay. Don't disappear. Let's go out this evening. There's a good Wine Bar in the next street. Luigi or Balugi or something. They had a turbot risotto on the menu last time I was there. Never heard of it before – really good. Come on, just for a good talk. I only ever seem to say a few words to you and we go our separate ways."

"What have we got to talk about? This has been an experience to forget" Lindsay replied.

"A glass of wine and you can tell me why you stopped playing."

"All right. I'm not dressed for a long evening."

"Come now. We can walk it in two minutes."

They were the first into Belugas that evening and took a small table beside the side window. Joel ordered a bottle of Chablis, noticing the predominance of fish on the menu. They were both ready for the cool crisp wine and drank the first glass before either spoke.

Joel looked at her and said "Why did you stop playing? It must have been a good living for another few years. You were still the best player in New Zealand weren't you?"

"Why do you want to know ? Nobody else cares."

"No-one else ? What about the different men I used to see you with?"

"They were the main problem. All good time seekers. Nothing long term came my way."

"Parents, family? Sponsors. 'New Zealand Tennis'?"

"Mum and Dad too preoccupied with their own trial separation and all the screwed up finances that go with it. Sponsors tailed off in direct ratio to my results tailing off. I am no longer on the Auckland Association radar."

"What about Doubles or Coaching? Surely better than a freelance reporter earning peanuts."

"Just needed a break from the round of playing and training and not eating and being bawled out by coaches and managers. Look, why do you need to know, anyway?"

"Call it the price of a meal."

"So you're not just after my body?"

"Was that on the table, then?"

"No, it bloody wasn't."

"There was a rumour about you and some bloke and a snooker table wasn't there?"

"I suppose that article was all around the locker room. It lost me one of my main sponsors. And it wasn't even true."

"Sounds uncomfortable."

"We were both pissed, having lost that afternoon and decided to play snooker for the prize of a cappuccino"

The strong wine was beginning to relax Lindsay. So Joel decided to get to the point before her thinking dissolved into a fog.

"I was talking to your old manager yesterday and he ………"

"Lazy Bastard!"

"He said nice things about you."

"Maybe he should have spent more time managing instead of trying to get inside my kit."

"Well, yes. That is not usually written into the contract."

"What did he say?"

"A lot. But one thing made me contact you. He said that you were more interested in living alone on a South Seas Island that succeeding on the tennis court. True or false ?"

Lindsay took two swallows of the wine.

"Are we going to eat something. I'm starving. I only had some fruit today, and that was mid-morning"

They ordered a seafood platter for two and some garlic bread.

"True. Since I was a kid I have wanted to leave behind all this materialistic society and get back to nature. You know, like the North American Indians or the Polynesians of old."

"Well. You may be surprised to hear that the only books I ever bought myself to read were stories of the explorers and adventurers of the Pacific. Everything the Norwegian Thor Heyerdahl ever did or wrote about I have read two or three times. And all about the discovery of some of the islands, the way of life. How they all got there and their customs."

"I am not so sure about cannibalism and screwing on the beach all day and night." said Lindsay loudly enough for the couple who had just arrived to decide to sit on the other side of the wine bar after all.

Joel picked up the empty Chablis bottle, looked at his companion, who nodded, and he waved it at the barman/waiter. The barman already had another one chilled and waiting in anticipation.

Their empty stomach linings had absorbed enough of the alcohol in the wine to fill the next twenty minutes with enthusiastic pronouncements of the virtues of natural living and remote island hideaways. Their food arrived to slow down the conversation.

"So what?"

"What do you mean 'So what'?"

"If you are not planning to add me to your list of conquests, why are we talking about my childhood fantasies?" Lindsay said with a mouth full.

"Perhaps I am scheming to take you out to some remote atoll and ravish you under a palm tree."

"Yeah. Great until the wind blows and a coconut falls on my head causing a fracture of the skull and the nearest hospital is 500 miles away across the sea, and all we have is a canoe."

"Your infectious optimism impresses me immensely"

"Tell me more about the ravishing bit." The wine was loosening her tongue.

Joel put down his fork.

"Crazy idea. I am in the middle of a bad run on court. You have given up Tennis, at least for the foreseeable. I have some money put away. We both need to get out of the range of these gambling thugs, who may decide to have a go at us. Just to be vindictive because we have put away their buddies. Let's pack a bag and bugger off to some island of your dreams and live off coconuts and fish and fruit for as long as it takes."

"As long as it takes for what?"

"As long as it takes for me to fall for your elusive charms and then you can get the next boat back to your new career as a tennis sleaze reporter."

"I don't write sleaze."

"Yes, you do. It's all speculation over relationships. Halfway between 'Hello' and the 'Sunday Mirror.' There's about as much tennis in there as there was on your snooker table."

"That's not fair. The editor chops my stories around. Look, are you serious about the Island or just mucking about with my emotions ?"

"Serious. Seriously serious. As serious as McEnroe said the umpire couldn't be! Let's do it. Let's go now. Don't analyse it too much.

Go home, pack a bag, write to the editor:-

'Dear Harold, Thanks for the job. I am taking a ten year sabbatical. Will call when I return. Love from Lindsay.'"

"What about Mother?"

"Bring her too. We can trade her for favours from the local chief."

"Maybe that's what she needs. Having been away from Dad for months. She will be OK here. In her bungalow and lots of new friends, mostly retired."

"She is used to you being away. Cats? Dogs? Budgie?"

"I only got Vanilla because I was based here all the time. I'll miss her but she'll be good company for Mum."

"What is Vanilla. An ice-cream machine?"

"Dog. Nice dog. Labrador."

"Nasty, smelly things. Just eat and crap all day. Useless."

"Stop it. You'll make me stay."

They finished the food and the wine and headed for the door. Joel paying by card on the way out. Lindsay leant on him as they walked out into the evening daylight. It was only 8pm. He hailed a taxi, put Lindsay in it and gave £20 to the driver to take her to her hotel.

"Meet you in the Beluga, with bag and ready to go at lunchtime tomorrow. Say 12.30. Don't change your mind, I'm booking flights."

The cab drove away without Lindsay replying. She sat in silence for a minute. Then the driver said

"He's worth going off with, then?"

Lindsay didn't answer. She sat back and thought. All she had ever wanted as a teenager was going to happen. Not another one of her many daydreams. It was going to happen tomorrow.

In the hotel room the effect of the Chablis was beginning to wear off. She took off her minimal make-up and washed her face with cold water before lying on the top of the bed.

'Can't be true. He's playing with you. All those promises from the past. Just men with stories to get you into some bed somewhere. Different stories because they thought that, after a glass or two of wine, you were too stupid to realise what their little game was. Always the same game. A ruse to exercise their best little friend. Some friend ! One that never made a commitment.'

She went to sleep, still in her outdoor clothes only to wake at 3.15am with a headache. Changing into pyjamas she began to put together the commitment that she had made the previous evening. It was all rather a blur. Was he serious? She would check that in the morning. Just in case he was she needed to prepare for a mammoth adventure. How can she do that in a day? Impossible. But he said he would book flights. This was all too much. Lindsay dozed and then went back to sleep.

She awoke again with a start. The sun was high and it was well into the morning. Her clock said 8.20am. She leapt out of bed and fell over the backpack that she had left beside the bed in the night when she had begun to think about the clothes she would need for this mythical journey to the Pacific. Breakfast was the last glass of orange juice in the carton. First job was to call Joel and catch him before he bought air tickets for today. Number, number? What is his number? Where is he staying? She didn't know. Oh God. How can I contact him? I need to check it's all true.

'I'll call Samuraja. He'll know where Joel is.' She called the London Tara Hotel and woke Sammy up.

"What do you want at this hour of the night ? I'm not giving you my life story ever."

He told her that Joel phoned him late last night and was put through to the Hotel Bar. He just wanted to know of an airline that connected Sydney with Honiara in the Solomon Islands. Sammy had told him to ring a travel agent. Lindsay calculated from this conversation that the whole thing must be genuine and not a practical joke on her. She panicked. She had to leave her room by 12 noon to reach the Beluga by 12.30pm, their arranged rendezvous. Three hours to pack and bale out of the hotel, give up her job and explain to her Mother.

Joel drew out a lot of money from his English Bank

Account, leaving a small balance. Enough to keep the account open. He took a taxi to a travel agent in Kensington High Street and bought two air tickets from Heathrow Airport to Sydney via Hong Kong, deciding to book the ongoing leg to Honiara in Sydney as the agent had no arrangement to patch them further into the Pacific Islands. He exchanged pounds sterling for some US dollars at the same agency.

The coffee date that he had arranged with Sammy the previous evening was early. At 10.30am they met in a coffee shop in the French Quarter near South Kensington tube station. Joel handed Sammy a large grip of tennis gear and two letters, one to his main sponsor and the other to his Manager. He apologised for backing out of their doubles team for the rest of the year. Sammy would have to find another partner. Sammy explained that, in the circumstances of the likely threat to Joel and Lindsay, he quite agreed that this was one of the best courses of action they could take.

"Come back soon Partner." was his farewell remark.

Joel picked up the other bag, a haversack that had been hastily put together in the morning, and disappeared into the tube station.

There was a phone box opposite Beluga Bar. Joel took the bag of coins from his pocket that he had been given earlier at the Bank and began to call friends, whose numbers he had in his blue pocket book. He began with Britt in Gothenburg, a long call. Then Monika, his mixed doubles partner for the last year. It was getting close to 12.30pm and Lindsay would be arriving soon. He could see across the road anyone entering the Wine Bar.

He then called the next hotel he was due to stay in followed by three more friends. They all expressed sadness but wished him well and a prompt return. It was now 12.50pm.

Joel put the remaining few coins from the telephone bag into his pocket and walked across the road to the Beluga. He stood in the doorway for a full minute and contemplated the prospect of living alone on the Island. She saw him from the bus window as it slowed for her stop.

"God. It's all true, she thought. He's there. He's waiting there"

Helped by the smiling off-duty driver, who was sitting near his colleague, Lindsay almost fell off the bus step as she tried to carry a heap of belongings. The bus pulled away to reveal a dishevelled Lindsay standing on the pavement in the middle of one bulging backpack, six or seven carrier bags, a winter coat, scarves and a jumper. She looked twice as wide as she had in the Wine Bar yesterday evening because she was wearing one hat and at least two of everything else. Joel came out of the Bar doorway and applauded from the other side of the street.

It took a few minutes to decant Lindsay into the Wine Bar and take up the entire area around the same table they had occupied last evening. She had thrown her arms around Joel

"You came. It's true. My dream wasn't a dream."

She hardly drew breath during the next ten minutes. Joel managed to glean from her excited monologue that she needed still to visit her Mother's home near Brighton and leave half of the clothes she was carrying with Mother. The flight was a late one and they had until 7pm to check in. Joel held up a hand and ran across the road, back to the phone box. Half an hour later an Avis Hire Car drew up and they left the driver to return to base by bus.

Mrs Curtis was making them tea at 3pm and cutting sandwiches for the journey. She had been used to Lindsay moving around the world from tournament to tournament, so this was not a huge shock. A big hug for Mum and Vanilla, and only the backpack as luggage, saw them drive away towards London again in time to catch the Quantas 747 later in the evening.

# SIX

"What will we do when we get there?" asked Lindsay in the small hotel on the outskirts of Sydney.

"Commune with nature and eat fruit." Joel was trying to clean his trainers with a toothbrush.

"Is that your only toothbrush?"

"I think there is another somewhere but you can borrow this one if your mouth is feeling rough."

"Oh. Yeah. Thanks very much."

They made plans to leave this expensive city as soon as possible and fly to the Capital of the Solomon Islands, Honiara. Quantas arranged for them to fly to Brisbane and then on to Honiara with Solomons Airlines in their new Boeing 737, purchased as part of a share deal with Quantas themselves.

"I have a surprise for you" said Lindsay, sitting next to Joel on the floor of their room in a tennis contact's house in Brisbane. Joel was searching brochures for the name of a hotel or guest house in Honiara.

"You probably think I am some useless woman who is going to be a 'baggage' for you throughout this adventure, or a slave of some kind.

"It had crossed my mind."

"Well, if you call this number, you will get my Auntie Joan who lives on the slopes of a small hill near Honiara where she retired two years ago after teaching little Solomon Islanders for three decades. She may even have a bed for me and a floor for you to sleep on. So there!"

"Aren't you a little star, Lindsay Curtis?"

He returned from the lobby phone to announce that they would be welcome at Auntie's home and that there were two spare beds available, all for the small fee of a jar of vegemite and an emery board.

"I agreed, but what is an emery board?"

"Woman's thing for rubbing the rough bits off the ends of your fingernails."

"That's a relief. I thought it may be a great piece of plywood to add to the luggage. Where do you get those? Waste of money anyway. I scrape the nail on a brick wall to trim it off."

Lindsay went shopping alone with a list of things she thought may not be available even on the big Island. Instructions not to buy too much were ringing in her ears in case the bags were overweight for the aircraft.

* * * * *

"Where are you going?" The strident voice of Aunt Joan echoed through the wooden house.

"Nalongo"

"Where?"

"Nalongo. It's the twin island with Nupani and still uninhabited."

"They thought I had flipped when I told all the relatives I was retiring here and not back to New Zealand counting sheep. But you two need to be certified. There will be nothing there except bloody palm trees, 100 degrees in the shade, jungle and sand. Probably wild pigs and dangerous creepies. OK, so you are married, but you'll soon be pissed off with each other's company and no-one to talk to unless you paddle for days to get to the other island."

"Married. We're not married! ". Lindsay retorted indignantly.

"Well, my girl. You will have to be before you can get a certificate to live together out there. This is a civilised society, not some 'screw everyone' American culture. It is a condition of tenure around here."

Lindsay looked at Joel, who was convulsed in laughter on the other side of the room. She looked back at Auntie.

"I am not marrying him."

"Why not? I would if I had the chance. He's OK to look at, quite clean. Probably rich. Passable sense of humour. If it doesn't work out you get divorced later and go off with half his cash."

"I'm saving myself for Mr. Right "

"Yes, dear. So am I. Sixty-three and still looking." said Aunt.

Joel came over and joined them.

"I thought this was a 'free love' culture."

"The bloody Christian Missionaries caught up with the South Pacific. It's all Church on Sunday and no getting together before marriage or God will cut off the offending parts. At least that is in the public eye.

After dark there seems to be a lot of running up and down the beaches and big smiles on the faces of all the young people in the morning. However I believe the Clergy sleep peacefully and their consciences are clear."

They were beginning to like this lady. She sat back in her tall whicker chair and laughed and laughed. Recovering, she said

"Now, come on you two. I'll arrange the wedding. Today is Thursday. Saturday will be good. Everyone likes a party at the weekend. Dottie and I will organise the food. You go and see the Pastor and say all the right things. It's unlikely he has anything else to do on Saturday, except his fishing. Come on, come on. If you want the permission to live on your island you must get a grip."

She leapt up and went out on the patio and started yelling for Dottie.

Joel and Lindsay just looked at each other. Joel shrugged. Lindsay said. "I don't think this was part of your plan."

"We need to go along with it to get the permission, and then we can take it or leave it later."

Lindsay thought 'you can't just take or leave a marriage'. It makes a mockery of the whole system, but she didn't say anything as she realised she would be in a winning situation whatever happened. Together they went to see the Methodist Pastor, who agreed to marry them in two days time.

Joan came up trumps. She was a witness at the traditional Solomons ceremony, bedecked everyone with flowers, took photographs and organised a feast for all the guests. It seemed that the guests were all her friends from the various clubs to which she belonged, from the Golf Club to the Solomons equivalent of the Women's Institute. She said to the Pastor afterwards that she won't need to entertain anyone at home for the next twelve months.

There were flowers everywhere and Lindsay wore a crown of woven flowers of rich colours and a dress borrowed from Dottie. The ceremony was conducted by the Pastor together with a local chief wearing a large necklace of porpoise teeth. Everyone sat on the ground for the feast which featured chicken, rice, vegetables and coconut milk as a main dish followed by puddings of tapioca and cassava. Being a Methodist ceremony only soft drinks were consumed until the Pastor left, when an amazing range of cans and bottles appeared from the guests to be distributed liberally until well after dark.

The flight from Honiara to Nendo was due to leave at 10am so the happy couple contained their natural desires in Auntie's spare room and just slept exhaustedly in each other's arms. A happy Aunt bid them farewell at the little airport as they boarded a Solomon Airlines Twin Otter to the island of Nendo or Santa Cruz, as it is known to the outside world. This was the smallest plane that Joel had ever flown in. There were four other passengers and the pilots were flying barefoot. They flew over several other islands for an hour and forty minutes before landing in sunshine at Nendo. A pickup truck with four seats took them to the Fatutaka Resthouse in the little town of Lata to await the next boat heading for Nupani. They sat on the verandah of the resthouse overlooking the sea and an orange sunset that was the stuff of holiday fantasy.

Joel observed that they had now slept in four different bedrooms together and neither had jumped on the other in the night. Lindsay was wondering whether she was not desirable enough for him, in view of the multitude of women Joel must have slept with in his 21 years.

"Husband. I suppose it is about time we consummated our marriage."

"What the hell is 'consummated'?" asked Joel.

"Bonking, Darling. Consummation means 'shagging'"

"Ah. I see. Lying back and thinking of New Zealand."

"You can think of New Zealand if you like, I shall still be deciding whether I wish to give my maidenhead to a randy swede who doesn't love me."

"I thought Maidenhead was a town in England."

"It is. I don't know what went on there in the Middle Ages, but it sounds as though some squire was out on the razzle."

"Wife. If we don't do it at all, does it mean we can annul the marriage after all this?"

"Probably. I think it is one of the requirements of a proper marriage."

"How about if we do it and tell everybody that we haven't?"

"No good. I'll tell the truth and then be entitled to half your loot and houses and cars and that toothbrush you use to clean your smelly trainers."

"In that case......." Joel put down his empty plate and climbed out of his whicker chair. He picked Lindsay up from her sitting position and carried her into the building. She squealed. He kicked open the patio door and carried her down the corridor and, with one arm locked around her waist, unlocked the bedroom door and walked her over to the bed, turned her around and kissed her as passionately as she could ever remember anyone doing before.. The halter necked shirt and tiny denim shorts were never going to be a challenging barrier to a rampant male, any more than her flimsy underwear. She had never quite understood how men managed to divest themselves of all their own clothes in practically one movement and thought they must practise it a lot at home with a stopwatch.. The smell and strength of Joel's fit body dissolved any resistance that she may have had as she lay on the top of the bed. She began to enjoy the feeling that his tennis-rough hands were creating over her naked stomach and legs. This was an accomplished lover and so it took only a very few seconds for her to submit to half an hour of paradise in paradise.

Afterwards she was watching a bird walking along one of the spars inside the bamboo ceiling and said

"You didn't give me any warning. You haven't once expressed any interest in me as a partner or as a lover before."

"No."

"How is it then I have just been the victim of your rapacious lust?"

"What is rapacious? Is it like 'consummating'?"

"Nearly. You are just a randy Scandinavian bully taking advantage of a young innocent girl who is only half your weight."

"I didn't hear you protesting a lot"

"It's hard to protest with a battering ram kissing your teeth back into your throat."

"I was only consummating our new relationship, like you suggested. Quite nice it was. We could do a lot of this consummating on our island."

"I'll consider it"

"You had better get your knickers back on quickly then because we randy Scandies can reload our weapons faster than most."

Lindsay jumped out of bed, grabbed her clothes and disappeared into the bathroom.

They had to wait four days before the boat, an old-fashioned trading schooner, could take them to Nupani. Once every two weeks it did a circular trip taking people and provisions to the outlying Reef Islands. It was 77kms as the crow flies from Nendo to Nupani, but their journey was destined to be nearly 300 as they had to call into other populated islands on the way.

"Can't we pay them more to go direct ?" offered Lindsay.

"No. They have goats on board for Lomlom and they need to be unloaded first." Joel had already discussed this with the Captain. It was 80kms North of Nendo. The two large backpacks were put into the one tiny cabin. It seemed that the crew and any other passengers would be on deck. Joel and Lindsay, having checked out of the Resthouse, were waiting on the quayside at the allotted time for departure still watching a variety of packages and crates being carried onboard or swung across by a mini-crane that was fixed to the quay. An hour after departure time the goats arrived. Six of them, together with two minders or goatherds. They were coaxed up the gangplank. At around 11.30am a family of four appeared with several bundles of belongings tied up with string and five minutes later two ladies unloaded a solid trunk from the boot of a very ancient taxi.

The Captain, who looked younger than Joel's 21 years, beckoned them on board, pointed to the bench seat under a canopy at the rear, and gave the instructions to the one other crew member to cast off. Danny looked as though he should have been at school instead of setting off across the ocean. He pulled in the lines from bow and stern and then joined the Captain in the wheelhouse.

Once this may have been a sailing schooner, but the rumble of a powerful Lister engine could be heard below and they moved across the little harbour at 5 knots more than the sign instructed them to keep to. It was dusk as they pulled into the lagoon at Ngawa, where the delivery for Lomlom was due to disembark. The crew tied up and headed for a house across the square, not to return. Joel walked around and along the docking jetty, watching the goat party leave and head across the square in a northerly direction. He had been told it was a night's walk to their new home or field on Lomlom.

It seemed to be the custom to leave the passengers to their own resources so Joel led Lindsay into a street off the square and to a house with tables outside, which he took to be a café of some sort. There was music playing inside and flashing coloured lights over the door. Within a few minutes a child appeared with two steaming bowls of a chicken stew and beans. The couple fell on these hungrily as they had not eaten since an early breakfast at the Resthouse.

All the other boat passengers had brought their own food, obviously used to the non-catering trading ships of the islands, and they had all been asleep when Lindsay tripped over a small boy lying beside the gangplank in the direction of their cabin, waking and incurring the wrath of the rest of the family. In two minutes they all were back asleep and Joel had quickly followed her to the refuge of the cabin. There was a narrow bed and a wash basin, two coat hooks and two wooden chairs. The bed had a thin mattress and there was a sheet folded but unironed on the bed. No pillow, no towels. Joel lay on the floor, leaving Lindsay the bed. It was a hard wooden floor but he was able to use his backpack as a pillow. Probably better than they would have to begin with on Nalongo.

As soon as the sun rose over the harbour wall the crew reappeared. The Captain was carrying a large enamel bowl full of papaya, pineapples, tomatoes, and breadfruit. The Mother of the family took out a knife and began cutting these all into bite sized pieces whilst her daughter offered the bowl around to everyone to help themselves. The Janita, as the ship was called, was already en route to cover the twenty kms to Nifiloli, where, the two ladies left them, together with their trunk of purchases. They continued to Pileni, and little Makalom, where the parcels had to be collected from outside the reef by an outrigged canoe with an outboard motor.

Night number two was spent at sea on the way to the last stop before reaching their destination. Two large crates and innumerable packages were offloaded at Nukapu, together with the friendly family, with whom they had now shared all their tales and prospects of adventure on Nalongo.

Now only the crew remained. The Captain told them that they had made up the spare 'weather reserve day' and would be at Nupani a day earlier than expected. The Janita was now due to arrive in the mid afternoon but, as the sea was running strongly today, it may take a couple of hours to negotiate the reef and get into the lagoon to unload their gear.

The entry to the lagoon was from the South East, nearer to Nalongo than it was to Nupani. The lagoon was huge, shaped like a triangle with the islands at each end of the longest side. They dropped anchor as close to Nalongo as the depth would allow and immediately saw three canoes heading towards them from a kilometre away, paddling from Nupani. Nalongo was small and quite flat with a knob of a hill of the West side. Nupani, in the distance, they could see was at least four times as large.

Captain Pete waited until the canoes arrived. Two had outriggers. They held a long discussion with Pete, pointing several times at both Nalongo and at the two adventurers with what Lindsay thought was incredulity. Pete spoke Pileni, the fringe Polynesian language that many of the outlying islands had as their main language. He asked the welcome party to take the couple, their two haversacks and the box of 'essential items' purchased in Nendo, the hundred metres or so to the Island. His parting remarks were to tell them that he would come by once a month, perhaps to deliver goods to Nupani or en route to another island. If they needed him, plant a tall pole in the sand on the East side of the atoll with a coloured shirt or similar on the top as a flag. He would then have to negotiate the difficult entrance through the reef for a definite reason.

By the time they had decanted from the outrigger canoes and collected their packs together the Janita was slowly creeping through the reef and then on out to sea. There were five people in the canoes. They stayed on board during the unloading, talking all the time. Then, laughing, they paddled away towards Nupani.

# SEVEN

Joel and Lindsay sat on the beach under wide brimmed hats and looked out across the big lagoon.

"It must be two kilometres between the furthest points" Joel said.

"Husband. I'm frightened." she replied.

"Don't think about it too much. Just pick out the good things like 'It's completely uninhabited.' 'There is lots of shade and trees and sort of jungle'. 'The lagoon will be safe to swim in and there must be a load of fish to catch and eat.' 'Fruit trees should be there in the jungle and I can see a lot of coconuts – though getting them may be tricky.' Let's get in the shade and make some plans."

First priority was to find the water source that they had been told existed and was first found by Admiral Edward Edwards in 1791. The atoll was only about 400 metres long and shaped like a kidney. The chunky end of the kidney rose up to a hill no more than 60 feet above sea level. The vegetation was lush all around the hill making Joel think that there could be a water supply of some sort there. They left their bags behind at the back of the beach, took their two machetes from the box and headed along the beach in the direction of the hill.

"Those islanders thought we were mad," called Lindsay from behind Joel, who was striding ahead.

"Yes. Well we probably are."

"Mad white people obsessed with colonial aspirations, out to colonise their peaceful island existence and bring them into the 20th Century."

"It will be 21st Century soon. No, they are not worried. They will look at us as potential purchasers of things they can catch more easily than we can. They'll let us starve for a few days and then spring up with all kinds of good things, like Sainsburys on a Thursday."

"Why a Thursday?"

"Isn't that the day when all the new things come into their shops?"

"Never heard that before."

They broke away from the beach and began to climb Mt. Joan, as Joel had named it after Lindsay's Aunt. The vegetation was quite thick and the machete was useful to cut a path through shrubs and tall grass that were fighting each other to reach good sunlight.

"Is there a doctor on Nupani?"

"Doubt it. There are only 100 people living in the village. There's probably a Priest of some Mission. They get everywhere out here."

"I went out with a vicar's daughter once." added Joel. "Atheist's perfect dream, you know. To have a vicar's daughter."

"I don't want to know about your oversexed teenage life. You told the Methodist Minister in Honiara that you believed in God."

"I did once. My faith dissolved when I was kicked out of the choir in Malmo for not having been christened."

"That was hardly your fault."

"No. Exactly. Destroys a person's confidence, that sort of treatment."

"Are you scarred for life?"

"Started me playing tennis, so that Vicar's got a lot to answer for on the Day of Judging."

"Judgment. It's Day of Judgment."

"How would I know? There's only one thing I know from the Bible. The parable of the ten wise virgins and the ten foolish ones."

"I'll bet every Swedish boy pays attention when that one comes up in class"

"Not every Scandinavian boy is obsessed with sex you know"

"I suppose it's only 97.5%"

They had finally reached the apex of the hill to find that there was an almost sheer drop down the western side. Lying on their fronts they looked over to see water flowing out of a fissure about twenty metres below and creating a small waterfall. At the base of the hill on this side there was a wide, flat rocky ledge approximately two metres above the breaking sea. Worn by the falling water and at the base of the waterfall was a pool of water that would be shaded under the hill for half of the day.

They felt quite elated as they descended, having found fresh water and a fresh water bath to swim in. At about the same height on the hill as the fissure in the rock they noticed that water was running in rivulets down through the vegetation away from where they had been climbing. That was why the plant life was so prolific, of course. Joel cut a big papaya fruit to take back to the beach and Lindsay found a coconut that had fallen and not split open. They worked their way around the beach to the ledge seen from above to find a pool that was over a metre deep and maybe two metres wide.

"Don't go washing your smelly socks in my bath water." she instructed.

"Bath in the lagoon. We need this for drinking, not contaminated by bodies and bath gel."

As they made their way back to the backpacks they decided that it would be good to find a spot near the water supply to live in and call home. The sun was setting behind Mt. Joan as they strolled along the firm hot white sand of the beach that ran almost continuously around Nalongo. Dark descended quite quickly as it does in the tropics and they devoured the large ripe papaya washed down with coconut milk, that was exposed with two cuts across the top of Lindsay's coconut with the machete.. There was sufficient dried seaweed and woody vegetation to gather and light a fire to give some light and warmth as night set in. There being no moon that night the sky revealed a mass of stars stretching from one horizon almost down to the other. A hollowed out space in the sand was lined with their blow-up double mattress and they just lay back and slept in the paradise that each had always imagined it was in the South Seas.

Lindsay got up early to find her torch and search for the mosquito repellent that she had bought in

Nendo. Bites were beginning to itch on her back and legs. A few minutes later Joel stood up and walked in the dark to the water's edge to relieve what he thought were sandfly bites by swimming in the lagoon. Sunrise found them sitting side by side on the sand scratching like two monkeys at the zoo.

"We need some sort of tent or house to keep out the sandflies or whatever they are" Joel said as he fitted hooks to the fishing line that was one of his Nendo acquisitions. Catching fresh water prawns in his hat, he attached one of these as bait. He then positioned himself on a rocky outcrop that was in the shadow of a palm tree and fished. He had no idea what he was fishing for until a shoal of fish, some 20cms long, swam by. He saw nothing else for an hour when a two metre shark nonchalantly drifted beneath his hook and bait. Absolute shock gripped him as he realised he had swum in the lagoon in the dark thinking that it was safe from anything predatory. Later Lindsay mentioned that there were crocodiles in the waters around some of the Solomon Islands.

"But it says in The Lonely Planet that they are only in the waterways near Honiara" retorted Joel.

"Hope the contributor was correct then" she threw back at him.

Lindsay had spent the day visiting the known papaya tree for more fruit and washing her clothes in the lagoon. These had dried on the sand in a couple of hours. Joel, however, had fished all day long without a single bite. He collected more prawns in his hat and brought these back for their evening meal. They ate these cooked and mixed with the flesh of the coconut followed by another 30cm long ripe papaya. Too late he remembered that he was going to arrange a shelter to keep out the sandflies. Instead they went to an area behind the beach on to a patch of long grass. Walking around and around the grass flattened into a carpet of soft grass stalks. With the inflatable bed on this they could lie and look up at the stars. Midway through passionate lovemaking Joel stood up yelping that something had stung him on his bottom.

"Something has just bitten off a piece of my ass" he cried.

Lindsay had enjoyed a number of lovers over the years but, as yet, none had left in mid-session, so to speak. She laughed out loud as she could see the out-line of Joel hopping about clutching his left buttock and trying to see what had attacked him.

They never did discover the culprit, probably an exotic insect with a penchant for European bottoms. Instead they retrieved the two sheet sleeping bags that Aunt Joan had made up for them and climbed into these for the night. It was very humid and the sheets made them sweat a lot. In the morning they discovered that any part of them that wandered outside the sleeping bag had been bitten and concluded that it was not sandflies but mosquitos that were feasting off their flesh. Lindsay vowed to cover herself with repellant tonight.

A great many of the plants growing were bamboo or tarai, which is a sort of thin bamboo. Joel began to cut three metre long pieces which he hauled to their chosen house site near the water pool and drove them into the sand with a heavy lump of rock. He then tied them close together to make them strong horizontally. Soon he had a wall. Meanwhile, Lindsay had resumed the fishing with a spinner attached to the hook that flashed silver in the water to look like a small fish. To her delight she caught three fat fish that looked like bream to cook over the evening fire.

To make a break from housebuilding Joel tried climbing palm trees to reach coconuts. He had watched a young lad shin up a palm tree in Honiara and throw down coconuts. The boy had used a strong thick piece of cloth in a figure of eight shape to place his feet in and then just pulled himself up with his hands, drawing his knees up behind him to allow his feet to grip the tree. This freed the hands to go to the next level, and so on. It looked easy. Joel chose a tree that had a clutch of coconuts under the palm fringe, but was bent out at a diagonal over the lagoon, thinking that, if he fell, it would be into the water. This is, of course, what happened. Several times. He reached two thirds of the way up the tree once and then rested exhausted for five minutes before falling into the water. The remedy came, when Lindsay cut the longest bamboo pole she could find. Joel climbed halfway up the tree and she passed him the pole from below. He managed to poke down six good sized coconuts which fell into the water, soon to be followed by Joel as well. Lindsay collected them, warily watching for the shark which seemed to be living in their private lagoon.

They now had food and drink from a natural source and felt very good. Their skins were turning a golden brown, interspersed by wheals of mosquito bites from the ravages of each night. The water pool was a delight. Cool and refreshing. They would wash in the sea and then sit in the pool to be dripped on by two thin streams of water that fell from above in a mini waterfall. It was shaded for around seven hours in each morning and, although the sun warmed the water after 1pm, the water falling on them remained much cooler after its journey from low down in the earth.

Joel completed the small house inside a week using only bamboo, strong plant roots and stems of parasitic creepers to bind the poles together and the spars for the roof to the tops of the poles. Lindsay wove strands of the tall grass into panels for sections of the roof, which would eventually be in two long pieces resting on the spars and rising to an apex. As she completed the first side it began to rain. Not just rain, but tropical rain of the intensity they had read about but never experienced. They grabbed the two backpacks and stuffed inside them anything they could see that needed to stay waterproof. Then, already drenched, they clambered underneath the long piece of roof, lying on the ground with the roof panel propped just above them on four improvised corner supports. The rain hammered down splashing them as it hit the ground beside the panel. They were already wet from the sudden early bursts that caught them before they could hide. Without moving much the two of them stayed under the roof for almost an hour, until the rain eased and then petered out.

"Amazing." Uttered Joel. "Your roof kept us dry under the heaviest of the downpour. That means we will have a dry cabin to shelter in."

The days had been getting more and more humid. Every exertion brought them out in beads of perspiration. They left off all unnecessary clothes. Joel wore just underpants and Lindsay topless in bikini bottoms. Not being embarrassed naked in each other's company they did not expect to meet anyone else unless they made some sort of raft and paddled over to Nupani. However an outrigger canoe appeared one morning with two teenage boys paddling it. Joel went to meet them as Lindsay ran to grab the other half of her bikini, which she eventually found suspended inside the cabin holding a fish and two mangoes. When she re-appeared the boys had pulled their canoe up the beach and were showing Joel it's contents. Enterprisingly they had brought an array of fish, tomatoes and a green veg that looked like kale. There was also a hammer made from a piece of iron cannibalised from an engine of sorts and an adze – a kind of back to front spade. Lindsay made positive noises and Joel negotiated a price for everything they had brought, paying in Solomon Islands Dollars, for which he had exchanged both pounds and US dollars in a Bank in Honiara. The boys were delighted and came to look at the cabin. They walked around it talking animatedly. Then one climbed a coconut palm to pull from the top metre long strands of an under leaf. Whilst up there Joel gesticulated for him to knock down another batch of coconuts. He came down with the same ease that he had climbed and the two lads went around the cabin binding the roof spars more tightly to the wall poles. The other boy went to Joel making 'wind' noises and signs so they worked out that the roof would have been unstable in a strong wind. Lindsay opened a coconut and they all drank the water in turn before, grinning, the boys set off back to Nupani.

The few words of English that one of the boys had spoken told Joel that the sharks in the lagoon were harmless and always small ones. It was safe to swim. That night, plagued still by mosquitos, they tried lying in the warm water at the edge of the lagoon using large flat stones to hold their heads above the water level and help sleep. It was a complete success in keeping away the mozzies but every time one of them dozed off there was a tendency to turn and find his/her face in the water. Each in turn crept out and on to the sand. There they discovered sandflies biting and small crabs trying to get into every orifice as they looked for new hiding places along the beach.

The next day they took as a holiday and discussed ways of keeping the mozzies at bay. It was becoming the only major problem they faced, and one that was niggling enough to become a big hazard to their long term plans. The sleeping bag was thin but hot and they always managed to become half uncovered in their sleep, offering biteable parts to the voracious mosquito. Also somehow they managed to bite through the material if one of their limbs was pressed against it from inside. The water was warm enough to sleep in. However an hour was the most either of them had achieved so far, and each time they finished up making love in the water, which was much more enjoyable and a first, at least for Lindsay.

"I read in Sydney about this guy who kept mosquitos away by covering himself each night with vegemite." she said.

"He must have slept alone, if only due to the smell."

"We could try it."

"Hardly. We don't have any vegemite."

"You mustn't let these small details put you off trying my suggestions."

They thought there were usually remedies for problems created by plants in another plant that grows nearby. Native tribes around the world had discovered this. Perhaps there were remedies for mozzy infestations nearby as well.

"Let's find anything in the plant line that smells and is likely to deter insects. Things that grow on the Island." Suggested Lindsay.

For the next week they covered themselves in every fruit and plant sap, flower essence and bulbous root that they could find or dig up, and went to bed for the night embalmed in each one in turn. None of them made the slightest difference. Mozzy ruled.

# EIGHT

It was becoming unbearable. Everything else was acceptable. Beyond acceptable. It was a delight to be there. They missed a few things, like cheese and Mars Bars and particularly Polo Mints, but it was a small price to pay for paradise. However things took a turn for the worse. Each was now finding a dozen or more new bites every day and, although it was better if they did not, the urge to scratch became a severe mental challenge. Their skin was becoming blotchy all over as the small poison from each bite created a lump until the immune system of their bodies dispersed it. On this day Joel's ankle became infected where bites had refused to heal and Lindsay used the first of the anti-biotics that were in the first aid pack. The fun was wearing thin as their thoughts became dominated by the condition of their skin and the prospect of the next night was more and more daunting. They even stopped looking forward to the chase and the culmination of their lovemaking.

"Husband"

"Mmmm"

"It's nearly a month since we arrived. We have

run out of mozzy repellant and I'm not sure it works anyway. We have tried every possible thing to fight them off and nothing has worked. I love the smell of your body, even your perspiration, but not when it is covered in some plant sap that stinks like chicken shit. Can we go somewhere which has all this island has, without the bloody insects?"

"Yes. Sure. Where?"

"I don't know. Another island where the mosquitos haven't landed yet."

"I think they got to all the places before people did."

"What about an air-conditioned container that is sealed as a bedroom and we can take around with us. Like on the back of a ship that we can moor beside the places we go."

"Nice idea. Would probably work. Got a million dollars handy to build it or buy it?"

"We could go back to tennis and earn it." added Lindsay.

"Do you want to go home?"

She looked across the pool of water that they lay in, in the shade and burst into tears.

"I didn't want to be the first one to back down."

"You aren't. I have been miserable for days now, but I didn't want to spoil your dream. We can't go on without proper sleep."

"Look at me," she said, "look at my lumps."

"I do. Most of the time."

"Not those lumps. These lumps. All up my arms, all over my legs and my stomach. Bites on bites. My hands itch so much I don't know where to scratch."

"I tied my red T shirt to the coconut pole yesterday,

in case Pete steamed by the Island. But I didn't want to hoist it without your complete agreement."

"I don't think I could go another month like this. Yet, I don't want to leave. It's the best time I have ever had, in the best place I ever went, with the best lover anyone ever had...................she tailed off with a sob......."

They hoisted the flag reluctantly at the farthest East of the Island and, two days later, Janita came through the narrow gap in the reef. This time Danny and Pete both came from the mooring in an inflatable dinghy.

"You just want to see us or you coming back with us."

"Coming back. Everything brilliant except the bloody mosquitos."

"No malaria here. You don't need to worry."

"Lindsay showed him her arms covered in red bumps and wheals."

"Shit. You must be allergic or something."

They silently put their bags in the dinghy, leaving the machete and the new tools in the cabin in case the next visitor needed them. The Janita motored slowly along the lagoon to Nupani, where they delivered two crates. It was hard to look at their Island as the coaster came back towards the reef entrance. Nothing was said. They both stood at the stern until Nalongo became a black smudge in the golden sunset.

They flew from Nendo to Honiara, Honiara to Brisbane and Brisbane to New Zealand.

"I'm going to see how Dad is getting on back in Otago. I think I may try teaching kids."

Joel flew with her, not quite sure what to do or where to go now.

"When we get to Auckland buy a ticket home. Best to go via San Francisco and back to Europe that way. No strings. It was great while it lasted. Go and earn the money for the ship with the container bedroom and give me a call when you've done it."

He bought her a packet of polo mints in Auckland Airport.

"Bye Husband."

"Bye Wife."

She didn't look back as she walked through the swing doors. The tears had returned with a vengeance

\* \* \* \* \*

The Air New Zealand flight from Auckland to Los Angeles stopped for an hour at Rarotonga in the Cook Islands. Looking out of the window as they came in to land reminded Joel of the very best parts of his and Lindsay's attempt to live on their South Seas Island. He remembered how resilient she had been to the rigours of life outside the luxurious walls in which 'westerners' spend most of their lives. He wondered why we did not spend more time going back to the basics of nature and grow much of our own food and spend spare time helping those who struggled under the weight of the challenges of raising a family and coping with illness. Sitting in the seat next to him was a girl of about thirty, who told him, on the second leg of the flight that she had started a home for destitute children in India a few years ago and now had twelve little ones to look after with limited resources. Currently they were continuing with the generous help of family members and friends.

They began to talk more widely about world poverty and whether there were too many people now living on the planet.

"If you stand all the people in the world shoulder to shoulder the area they would cover would be no more than the area of the city of Los Angeles." said Kate.

"OK" answered Joel "Why then can't we grow enough food on the rest of the earth to feed everyone?"

"The problem is not lack of space or lack of good agricultural land it is poverty itself. Poor organisation and poverty. Many people are too poor to be able to own land, or be able to get water or seed for the land they do own. They are trapped in a social network where much of the land is owned by a few wealthy people who demand rents that mean the farmer has to sell all his crops to pay. There is often not enough left to improve the land and grow more next year. Often there is not enough left to buy even the seed to continue farming."

"What is the answer?"

"To me, it is so simple. Educate everyone that there are sufficient resources in the world to feed all the people well, not just some well and the rest so badly that they live miserable lives and die early. Then the United Nations Organisation has to get its act together really well and take a full lead in setting an example, country by country, of guiding the governments to distribute the fertile land evenly amongst the population who wish to farm it. They need to finance water systems and harvesting equipment, help with pest control and distribution of the crops. Many countries are doing this quite well. The UN should use the experience of these to clone the ideas and have them spread around the globe. In the West we apparently throw away 30% of the good food we buy through extravagance and bad habits or bad planning. This is terrible and future generations will look back at us with horror."

They disembarked at San Francisco and were transitting on to two different airlines. They shook hands and Kate said

"I know who you are because I watch a lot of tennis when I can. Give my Sammy a hug for me when you see him." She smiled and walked off in the direction of a flight to London.

Joel stood in the arrivals hall speechless. He had spent all that time sitting next to the nearest that his best friend had to a mother without suspecting it. On his next flight, this time with SAS Scandinavian Airlines, he thought a lot about Sammy and how he had been helped to climb out of destitution to compete in the lucrative world of sport. Sammy was putting some of his earning back by building the Children's Home stronger for others to follow. Maybe he, Joel, could do something similar.

Joel was greeted warmly by Britt and his sister Anya, who had become engaged to be married in a few weeks time. He began to play golf and to have lessons with the professional at the Gullbringa Golf Club in Gothenburg. Playing every day he quickly improved to a single figure handicap. One Saturday, playing in a fourball, the other three ganged up on him. On the fourth tee they told him in strong terms that he was an idiot to be out there with them. While still young he should be waving the gold and blue Swedish flag on a tennis court. They told him to pack a bag that evening and go to the very next tournament and sign on. They did not want to see him on their golf course again until he had won at least two Grand Slam events. Joel left them, that evening, still laughing.

Deep inside the tennis bug stirred and he emailed Sammy to meet up when he next came to Europe. In the meantime he found an indoor court in Gothenburg and began practising with the local professionals, alternating with intense periods in the gym. He and Sammy met later in the month. Since Joel had gone back to nature Sammy had enjoyed considerable success in doubles. He had decided to become a doubles specialist and to try to emulate the Woodies (Todd Woodbridge and Mark Woodforde) who were winning tournaments, cash and sponsorship in every direction. There was a doubles event, running parallel to the singles at every major tournament and, although the prize money on offer was considerably less than at singles, there were relatively few players who concentrated principally on this form of tennis. The tournament organisers and sponsors however knew that the public enjoyed and often actually preferred watching the doubles for the competitiveness and the speedy rally exchanges at the net.

Sammy's partner, Christian from Norway, had damaged a finger in a bad fall when he had collided with the wooden netpost. It needed an operation and would take several months to heal properly. It was on his right hand, his racket hand, and so his effective tennis was over for this season. Sammy, without checking Joel's current fitness, offered Joel the replacement position for the next few months at least. It would break him back into competitive tennis again gently. He could resume his singles game later when he felt ready. This was attractive to Joel, who was missing the fun and the camaraderie of the circuit as much as the tennis itself. They began playing together and progressed a couple of rounds in each of the first two tournaments. Joel enjoyed this format and the banter that often went with it, so he decided to find his old mixed doubles partner Monika and encourage her to team up for a trial event.

Although Monika was an aloof individual she had been in love with Joel for the last two years. She was the daughter of Danish Government Minister, Jan Kristensen, and carried herself with an air of superiority. She was tall and played gracefully. Her groundstrokes were elegant and her height gave her excellent reach for net play. They won the very first tournament after they were re-united and this sealed the partnership for the rest of the season. Monika hung around Joel every evening in the competitor's hotel longing for a close personal relationship. The Press had begun to suspect this and were constantly enquiringly about their friendship. Monika refused to answer any of their questions and detested press publicity because her father had been vilified once in the political columns unjustifiably. She became known as unco-operative so the reporters made up stories about her and referred to her as 'the Snooty Beauty.' Trying to protect her from a particularly persistent photographer, who was waiting in the foyer of the hotel Joel suggested that she stayed longer than usual before calling a cab to her own accommodation. They had both had quite a lot to drink when the rest of the party had been celebrating someone's success and finished up trying to hide in Joel's room. The photo of her leaving his room appeared in the sleaze pages of the Sunday Newspaper with the expected text.

A friend showed this to father Jan in Denmark, who told his daughter that he expected to hear of an engagement between the couple in the near future to preserve the dignity of his office as a high ranking Danish Minister.

"We need to be engaged." Monika greeted Joel as they both appeared for practise the next morning.

"The only engagement we need is to turn up for the first round of the Madrid Open on Tuesday." replied Joel.

"Father may withdraw his support. He read that article in the paper on Sunday."

"What support? Turning up to watch twice a year and press interviews to tell them what a star you are. Tell him to concentrate on his own affairs."

"He doesn't have affairs. He is loyal to my Mother."

"He is Minister of Foreign Affairs. That means he has affairs with foreign men and women."

"Those are different affairs." Monika retorted angrily

"We couldn't live together. We would always be fighting. Let's just play tennis together where the union works and not push our luck "

They did not exchange any more words until he received a phone call from a scared Monika in his hotel room in the mid afternoon.

# NINE

"Let go, let go…………Joel is that you? They say they are going to break my arm to stop me playing. They wanted me to tell you……………"

The phone was handed over to someone else.

"Joel Eriksson ? This is Oscar. We met before. You had my mates sent down."

"That was the Police."

"All right. If you were not involved you can now show us your loyalty. We've got your girlfriend and we're going to hurt her unless you do what we say."

Joel heard Monika shout "Please Joel, help me"

"You want more input into your gambling scam, I suppose."

"Yes. A lot. Something in every game you play or she suffers."

"OK. Let her go and I'll do what you want."

"Any backsliding on our instructions and we will collect her and bust her arm so bad she won't play again."

"Let her go and tell her to call me in ten minutes to tell me she is safe."

"We will meet you at your hotel 10am tomorrow." Oscar rang off.

Monika phoned Joel's room a few minutes later saying she was safely released and asking him what this was all about. He told her it was a crooked scheme involving tennis, but no more information for her own safety.

"You will do what they want."

"Don't you worry about a thing. I'll sort this out once and for all."

Joel sat on the bed and tried to work out how he should react to this latest approach from Oscar.

The 'We' on this occasion turned out to be Oscar and a heavy called 'Pony' although Pony looked more like a shire horse at around 20 stone and six foot four. Oscar demanded the same type of actions from Joel for people 'spot' betting overseas. Joel agreed to do what they said. The first was the old double fault, to be in his first service game in a men's double two days later. The next turned out to be difficult. He was to 'foot fault' in a mixed double that he was playing with Monika. True to the arrangement Joel served with his foot well over the service line. The linesman, a young man, didn't notice and so nothing was called. It was already forty-love now, so Joel tried again. Again the line judge missed the error. Someone in the crowd even said 'foot fault' in a loud voice, but it was too late. They won the point to finish the game. Joel was not too concerned because he had played his part and couldn't be penalised for the poor line judging.

The same evening his room phone rang and it was Monika in tears. She was calling from a hospital in the centre of Barcelona, where the tournament was being held, having just had her arm set in plaster. The two thugs had forced their way into her room, twisted her arm behind her back and broken the bone, telling her that this was a message to Joel for not doing as he was told and costing them $20,000.

"You could see in the TV coverage that I did what you wanted." Joel explained to Oscar on the phone the next morning. He knew it was too late to do anything about Monika's chances of playing again this summer. However he resolved to turn Oscar in to the Authorities at the first opportunity. This time he went to the Malaysian Embassy in Barcelona and had an audience with the Ambassador, who in turn contacted a senior officer in the fraud dept. of the Kuala Lumpur police. Together, two days later, they set up Oscar in Joel's hotel room with recording equipment fixed under a table and the Malaysian and a Spanish detective waiting outside the door to arrest Oscar as he left the room.

Monika's problem was not as bad as Joel had feared. Pony, knowing nothing about tennis, had broken her left arm. Although she was somewhat traumatised by the whole experience and began constantly looking over her shoulder to see whether she was being followed it did enable her to keep practising most of her game. Service was difficult. The weight of the left arm plaster making it impossible to throw the ball up accurately. She made no secret of the fact that she thought Joel now owed her his full attention as a companion as well as tennis partner. Joel felt guilty and decided to pay her 10% of his winnings to compensate in a small way for her injury and new fears.

These events coincided with Joel's tennis improving rapidly. He had never particularly enjoyed playing the clay court season, his preference was always for grass or asphalt surfaces. However he began to rise in the ranks, reaching the top ten for the first time by making singles semi-finals in Italy and in Monte Carlo, and again in the French Open at Roland Garros, where he had two match points to get to his first singles final for over two years. At the same time he and Sammy discovered that their doubles partnership was working exceptionally well. Sammy had become a doubles specialist where he found that his net and overhead game was more in use than in singles. Both in doubles with Joel and mixed with good partners he was achieving success and making a good income.

Joel and Sammy won the French Grand Slam doubles and partied all Saturday night in Paris, making sure that Monika was also there to keep her spirits up. The plaster was due to be removed from her arm on Monday and she was looking forward to being able to play without the weight on her left arm. She had been practising hard during her lay off and working in the gym with her coach. Her singles ranking had slipped badly whilst she could not compete and she was anxious to climb back to the ranking that would secure invitations to all the principal tournaments for the remainder of this year and for the next.

The news that Oscar had escaped from custody in Barcelona was brought to Joel as he prepared for the first of the grass court tournaments of the summer in the South of England. He was not particularly worried. It delayed his having to go back to Spain to give evidence in the case against Oscar and 'Pony'. Pony was convicted alone and sent to prison for three years for grievous bodily harm to Monika. Monika was spared an appearance in court as Pony had partially confessed to the crime. He also had a record of violent assaults in two other European countries.

Samuraja, coming from the sometimes violent society of India, was more concerned for Joel's safety than Joel himself. Sweden was a peaceful country with few guns and below average violence of all kinds. The potential threat from Oscar seemed small to Joel. Oscar was probably without passport, somewhere in Spain, dodging the police. Joel was in England with plans to play two tournaments before Wimbledon taking up the whole of June. Sammy persuaded Joel to agree to find an anonymous place to go during the rest of the summer until the revenge subsided in Oscars mind and Oscar resumed his criminal activities elsewhere. They took a day out and went down to the Hamble River near Southampton to enjoy themselves and look at boats. The visit led to them buying a Benetteau Evasion 32 , a sleek white ketch that would be fun to sail. Both had spare money in the Bank from recent doubles successes. Every rest day they had in June was spent on the Solent with Harry, a sixty year old retired carpenter, whose hobby had been sailing since he was a boy. They each learnt how to sail quite proficiently and continued back in their hotels reading avidly on the subject. It was a complete change and a relaxation from tennis and Sammy had a plan to put into effect after Wimbledon and in the two month gap before the US Open in September.

Meanwhile Monika was able to work on her service now that the left arm had healed and the plaster cast was removed. She was able to throw the ball up accurately with her left hand to be met by the racket swung smoothly by the right hand. Service was one of her best assets and her height helped the trajectory of the ball to travel directly down to a twelve inch segment of the receivers service line. She served many aces, a rarity in the women's game and an especially useful addition to the doubles matches. Her principal successes to date had been in ladies doubles with her Czech partner Jelena and in mixed doubles with Joel. She and Joel were seeded four at Wimbledon and beat two dangerous wildcard entrants in the early rounds. Due to rain delays they found themselves playing two rounds in each day late in the second week of the Tournament.

Meanwhile Sammy and Joel had reached the quarter finals of the Men's Doubles, only to be beaten by the second seeds, Bhupati and Paes, another specialist doubles pairing in the quarter final. With Samuraja on Court as well it was unusual to have three competitors from India playing together in a Grand Slam event.

Joel and Monika reached the Final that was the last match to be played on Centre Court on the final Sunday. They were up against the first seeds who included Maria Palatti with her ferocious, but wild forehand. In an earlier round she had almost decapitated an umpire causing the male locker room to give her the nickname of Buffy (Buffy the Umpire Slayer). Buffy hit some fine forehands across the Court and down the line, but they were more than matched by Monika's service and her determination after the enforced early season layoff. Joel and Monika only lost one service game all match, which led to the loss of the second set. However they triumphed in three sets and were presented with their trophies in the Royal Box a few minutes later.

Sammy appeared as soon as the Press interviews were completed with a large bottle of champagne and Monika began to smile for the first time since before Barcelona. During the meal out that evening Sammy put his plan to Joel. He explained his concerns that the gambling syndicate may still be determined to gain revenge on Joel and that he should disappear for as long as possible, at least until Europol had caught Oscar. His idea was that they should take the new yacht along the English Coast or across the Channel to France and Joel should relax in a quiet cove and continue the painting that he enjoyed so much. He, Sammy, would be going to holiday and keep up his fitness in Majorca and would spread rumours that Joel was out there with him or somewhere on the Island.

Monika was involved in this and, listening from the fringe, decided that she should go with Joel as well. The two men caught each other's glances and both left the celebration planning an escape that would be without Monika. Joel left her a note to wish her parents well from him and that he would see her in New York in September. He slipped away early the next morning and met Sammy in the hotel car park.

# TEN

"I didn't think you wanted to have too deep a relation-ship with her,". said Sammy.

"Not really my type off the court." Replied Joel.

They headed for Southampton, stopping for break-fast at Winchester Services on the M3. The weather was overcast with drizzle and sea mist likely today. It was not good for sailing so they spent the rest of the day on board talking to Harry. He suggested making an itinerary along the coast to the West and mooring each night in one or other of the marinas that now dotted the South West Penninsula. It would be better to have had some more experience before tackling the Channel and the coast of France. They bought supplies and extras for the yacht from the Hamble Yacht Chan-dlers and settled into the bunks for the night.

The next morning was bright and clear. The sun rose early as this was the time of year when the days were longest. They checked the radio and advised the Har-bourmaster that they were leaving and heading West towards the Needles. It was a lovely fresh morning and the two friends wondered why they hadn't been sailing before in their free time. They were wearing thick sweaters against the gentle south-westerly breeze that greeted them head-on as they pointed down the Solent towards Yarmouth on the Isle of Wight. As the morning progressed they sailed past Hurst Castle and the Needles and onwards approximately a mile offshore past Bournemouth and the Isle of Purbeck towards Portland Bill.

"Where is the best place to call in for a break" asked Sammy

"They pulled out a chart and decided that Durdle Door/Lulworth Cove would be pleasant to drop anchor and find somewhere to buy a meal or, considering their inexperience, perhaps the jetty at Weymouth may better. Joel went below to use the small onboard toilet that neither of them had yet tried. As he stepped into the cabin the door closed behind him. He looked around because he hadn't touched it to find himself looking into the face of Oscar, who had one hand on the door and a kitchen knife in the other.

"Been waiting for you to come down here," said Oscar. "We have a score to settle, or two or three"

Joel was thinking quickly. There was no point in calling Sammy who couldn't leave the steering to assist. He needed some protection from the knife so he grabbed the thick cushion from the seat beside him.

"Got the wrong arm of your girlfriend but I know you are right-handed and I can slow down your progress if I cut you well"

"What will you gain by that, Oscar? More time on your sentence when they catch up with you."

"No-one has caught me yet and, with this boat, I'll get clean away"

He lunged at Joel who pushed the cushion against the knife and Oscar fell past him into the cabin. He turned quickly, still holding the kitchen knife with its blade upwards.

"Time to pay back, Mr Tennis Player"

He lunged again towards Joel's midriff. This time the knife came through the cushion missing Joel's leg by an inch. Whilst the knife stuck for a moment he grabbed the coffee pot they had used earlier and hit Oscar a glancing blow across his head. Coffee spilled all over his face and coffee beans spread into his hair. Oscar pulled the knife out of the cushion and paused. He came at Joel again with arms spread wide. Joel kicked him hard between the legs encountering something squishy that caused Oscar to yelp with pain and double up. Joel quickly opened the door and went up on deck calling to Sammy that Oscar was on board.

They watched as Oscar climbed gingerly out of the cabin, still holding the long knife in his hand. By now Joel had a wooden stave used for stunning fish and Sammy had one hand on the wheel and the other holding a piece of rope with a metal carabiner attached that had been lying near him on the deck.

"Pack it in Oscar," said Joel. "You can't beat both of us."

"I'll get both of you bastards and the boat. You've cost me a lot of money when I offered you a good deal, and now I've got half of Europe looking for me."

He jumped a foot along the deck and took a swing at Sammy. Sammy overbalanced backwards pulling the wheel towards him. Oscar stood over him leering with his arm raised. The movement of the wheel took the bow of the yacht through the wind, emptying the sail of air until the wind quickly snatched it from the other side. The boom swung across. Joel ducked as it whistled above catching Oscar on the back of his head. The knife fell on the deck with a clatter as Oscar grabbed at nothing and tumbled over the side into the sea. The yacht had taken the wind and was reaching away in the direction of land at about five knots before Sammy could get back on the wheel to correct it.

"I can't swim very much" came the cry from a now quite distant Oscar."

Joel unclipped a lifebelt and threw it as hard as he could in Oscar's direction. It was a long way short of the struggling man. Oscar's clothes were now saturated and the weight of these and his shoes was beginning to drag him down. As quickly as he could Sammy turned the yacht so that it ran before the wind in the general direction of Oscar. The lifebelt was floating a good thirty yards from the bobbing head. By the time it had taken the yacht to run back close to Oscar he had disappeared under the surface. Joel stripped off and dived in at the spot where he had last seen him and duck dived several times to try to get a glimpse of Oscar, while Sammy manoeuvred the yacht eventually back to where they were. Joel had now hold of the lifebelt and was leaning on it exhausted. There had been no sign of Oscar since he went under.

"He must have just sunk." Called Sammy.

They sailed up and down trying to see some sign of Oscar's body or clothes.

Joel told the whole story to Sgt.Watkins of the Weymouth police after they had moored and gone straight to the Station to report the incident.

"We went round and around, but there was nothing to see."

"Happens sometimes. Bodies just sink. They come back to the surface eventually but it can be days later." said the policeman.

He handed over the details to the CID as there was the implication of all sorts of crimes involved and the two friends were asked to stay in Weymouth until reports had been completed. Two days later they set off to the West again feeling subdued and a little guilty. They had been told that they probably would have to return for the Coroner's inquest. Neither of them had been around someone who had died before and were not sure how to feel.

They sailed across Lyme Bay turning into Lyme Regis harbour to moor and look around.

"The French Lieutenants Woman stood on that jetty over there." Said Sammy.

"How do you know that?"

"I come from India. We know everything ! Read it in a book when I was at school"

"What. About Lyme Regis?"

"Yes. It's a classic. They probably didn't bother to translate it into Swedish. Too advanced for your lot."

They sat outside eating a pub meal and watching the holidaymakers on the beach.

"Where are all the children?" asked Sammy

"Still in school I expect. The summer vacation hasn't begun yet."

They climbed back on board and motored out of the harbour, hoisting the sails as soon as they were clear of the jetty.

"The old guy sitting at the bar in the pub suggested we stay in Seaton Harbour overnight. I told him you were looking for a quiet place to sit and paint for a few weeks and he reckoned that that area is the best kept secret around here. Quiet harbour. Village pub nearby. Not too many grockles. His word for holidaymakers. Good things to paint. What do you say we go over and look. It's only a few miles along the coast. Next inlet."

"OK. This is your idea really. To hide me away whilst you are chasing all the best women in Majorca."

"Of course. I can't compete with you and your blond Swedish looks. What did Lindsay call you ? A randy Scandy wasn't it?"

"Not done much randying lately"

"This could be your big chance. All those well built farmgirls who wait all winter to meet someone like you."

They dropped the sails outside the mouth of the River Axe and motored gently into the estuary and a harbour area that was between a road bridge and the sea. There was a boat maintenance warehouse and the usual attendant debris around it, seven or eight larger vessels moored in the middle of the river mainstream and a number of dinghies and tenders pulled up in the car park or tied to the side of a pathway alongside the river. They motored up to a small jetty and were met by two men who could be father and son, and who came out of the maintenance shed.

"Can we moor up for the night?" asked Joel

"Yes boy. Take the orange float out in the middle. He's away to France for a couple of weeks. Five quid a night all right"

"Fine thanks. I'm Joel, this is Sammy."

"George Mercer and Phil". Was the reply. "Anything you need for the boat, give us a shout."

They moored and also tied into the line to save swinging in the tide.

"Let's tidy up and wander around. Makes a change from all the noise and hassle of big towns."

It was the first time they had used the inflatable and fiddled around with a small compressor to blow it up. Then they paddled it to the side, having changed their clothes into something less seagoing. The walk alongside the river on the other side of the little road-bridge was delightful and they drank in the sounds of the feeding and wading birds, of which there were dozens on both sides of the central river stream. An old tramway ran along beside the far riverbank which still operated as a holiday ride inland to a town five miles away. There was a golf course on top of the hill on the side they were walking.

"I could quite like it here." said Joel

"Good. This then is your hideyhole whilst the dust settles on Oscar and his mates find someone else to annoy". decided Sammy. "I'll zoom off to Majorca and anyone who asks will be told that you are somewhere up in the hills around Deya painting and relaxing."

They strolled into a village that was only half a mile along the river. There was an old coaching inn, a smart restaurant and four small shops. Back at the yacht the two friends settled for the night. The peaceful lap,lap,lap of the water on the side of the boat was soporific. They were only woken by the seagulls squawking on the foredeck. They ate a good breakfast at a café no more than a hundred yards from the harbour and had a good laugh with the very gay owner.

George Mercer took the five pound note and told them they could stay as long as they wanted. When the owner of the mooring returned they could move on to another. There was bound to be one free all the time. Sammy packed his grip and Joel walked him to the Jurassic Coast Bus Stop in the middle of Seaton. He would go to Exeter and then get a fast train to Paddington en route to Heathrow Airport.

"One last thing. It's unlikely you will be recognised down here in the wilds of the South West of England but, to be on the safe side, change your name. Leave Joel behind and become............Anders.........no, Erik, become Erik to everyone down here. Go on, do it. It's for the best in case anyone comes after you. Even Monika, ha ha.". The bus came by and Sammy waved from the top deck with a thumbs up gesture.

Four days later Erik caught the same bus at the same time, the train to London and a taxi to the Porsche Sales Centre in West London. He collected the white Porsche 911 that he had ordered three weeks before from Germany and gently drove it through the traffic of the city. He only opened up on the M3 and along the A31 through the New Forest. His new palette and box of tubes of oil paints on the passenger seat. He had a sixth sense that this was going to be a special summer for 'Erik' in a special place.

# About the Author

Stuart Neil lives in East Devon. He played tennis at Junior Wimbledon and was a Scotland Hockey International. For many years he has led Emergency Medical Teams for European Charities working in crisis zones in Asia and Africa.

He has finally succombed to the temptation to write and the novella *'The Tennis Racket'* leads into his 'Erik Trilogy':-

*'Second String to a Tennis Racket.'*
*'The Marbella String Quartet.'*
*'The Court Jester'*

Three romantic ventures into the world of Tennis and Ladies Golf.

Each of these books or the 'Erik Box Set' may be purchased through the Amazon website.

Printed in Great Britain
by Amazon